My First Ten Days
In Heaven

Also by Robert Brown

Simply Bob: Searching for the Essence (a memoir)
Personal Wisdom: Making Sense of You, Others and the Meaning of Life
Things I Learned From My Wife (a memoir)
Kids Character Building Toolkit
Invivo (a novel)

The HST Model for Change
The Dark Matter and Dark Energy of Lean Thinking
The People Side of Lean Thinking
Transparent Management
Earn Their Loyalty
Mistake-Proofing Leadership (with Rudy F. Williams)
New Darwinian Laws Every Business Should Know (with Patrick Edmonds)

A Thousand Rounds of Golf
The Golfing Mind
Mayhem at the Open (a novel)
Murder on the Tour (a novel)
The Way of Golf
The Golf Gods

My First Ten Days
In Heaven

Robert Brown

Denro Classics

Requests for permission to use or reproduce material from this book should be addressed to:
books@collwisdom.com

This is a work of fiction. The thoughts, feelings and actions of the characters are fictional and in no way reflect the person's true thoughts, feelings and actions.

Cover image by Reimund Bertrams, DasWortgewand, Pixabay

Published by Denro Classics
1700 Mukilteo Speedway #201-1084
Mukilteo WA 98275
USA

ISBN-13: 978-0-9836768-3-6
ISBN-10: 0983676836

Library of Congress Control Number: 2016921119

To people everywhere; may Heaven be
your destiny.

My First Ten Days in Heaven

This is a work of fiction and makes no claim of any theological representation of the afterlife. However, it does attempt to make better sense of life and death.

Contents

Home is the place where, when you have to go there, they have to take you in.
Robert Frost, "The Death of the Hired Hand"

Day
1

Being Dead

I'm afraid to open my eyes. The bed is soft, as if I'm swaddled in a giant down pillow and I feel better than I have in years. If I open my eyes, I will be in the hospital. In my hospital room, in my hospital bed, in my hospital gown, my body connected to machines with wires and tubes. With my eyes closed I'm in a safe, comfortable cocoon.

Must be early morning, it's too quiet to be anything else. But I don't recall getting my midnight meds. My back isn't sore. My legs and arms don't ache. Breathing is easy and relaxed. Maybe I'm dreaming, but I'll take it until the nurse enters carrying reality on a tray full of vials and needles. No need to open my eyes. What would I gain? I would lose everything I'm enjoying right now.

How long can I keep my eyes closed? All day if I want to. Until Beth or the kids come. I miss the grandkids, but I agree I'm a bit scary looking these days. I don't think I'm going to die this time; not this time, could be next time. I'm strong, weak physically, yeah, but not that weak and I refuse to give in. A person's spirit makes a difference and I'm not done yet, I'm not even close to being finished.

I should open my eyes, can't lie here daydreaming all day, if that's what I'm doing. As a good patient I have obligations: taking my medicines, clearing my lungs, moving around, getting the blood flowing. Shouldn't wait for the nurse; must take responsibility for myself. I don't have to pee. Can clear my lungs anytime. Temperature is perfect; it's usually too cold in here. I'm sure I'm awake and not dreaming; I feel good for once. Would I feel lousy again if I open my eyes?

Wait until the nurse appears. Come on, you're a grown man, face it grandpa, an old grown man. Open your eyes, behold the wonders of medicine, rejoin your dwindling world. Could still be night, hours of sleep left. If it's early morning you can witness the hospital begin its day.

I open my eyes. The room has changed. It's not my room. It's three times the size, light green rather than light blue. I begin the struggle to sit up but there is no struggle. I twist around and adjust the pillows with ease. Must scope out the new room. A queen size bed rather than a hospital one. A sofa rather than a heart monitor and two easy chairs, a kitchenette off to the side with a dining table and four chairs. The sofa is a light-hearted tweed of blues and grays and the chairs a darker solid blue. I get it. This is a room for visiting VIPs. They needed my room for someone else and I was moved into a suite that was vacant. When did that happen? No wires. No tubes. Doesn't even smell like a hospital; fresh, more like Hawaii, near the ocean. Now I'm sorry I didn't open my eyes earlier. Pajamas, I'm wearing pajamas. When did I get those? My memory is getting really bad if I can't remember putting on PJs. I'm probably going home today. Feel great, ready to go. No clock in this new room. Early morning, has to be. I'll be discharged around ten is my guess. Beth will be here to push me out in a wheelchair, I'll pop in the car at the hospital entrance and we'll be home by one. Home by one sounds great. I hope it isn't cold outside.

A soft knock on the door.

"Come in."

A nice-looking fellow enters the room, somewhere between the kids and grandkids' ages. He isn't wearing a uniform, so he's unlikely medical. Administration of some kind. Dressed relaxed, as I like, in khakis and a polo shirt, dark green, my favorite. He's wearing running shoes, though his extra bit of suet around the middle suggests they're more for comfort than jogging down the street.

"Good morning, Mr. Greyson. How are you today?"

"I am great. Better than in a long time. You guys do good work. What's the plan?"

"The plan, sir, is to get you situated. I trust you see your room has changed," he says, now standing next to the bed.

"Yes. Have no idea when that happened, but I'm happy it did."

"And you're feeling well?"

"Absolutely. I'm ready to get home and get busy again."

"Well, Mr. Greyson, there is good news and bad news. My name is Pete. My job is to guide you through the good and the bad."

"I feel great, that must be the good news. What's the bad, insurance isn't covering the hospital bill?"

The new guy Pete laughs. A nice, friendly laugh. I like him.

"No, nothing like that. What's the last thing you remember from yesterday?"

I search my memory for a moment or two. I remember my family visiting. Beth and the kids.

"My family visited yesterday. They do all the time. Visiting me might even be the highlight of their day."

He laughs again. "The bad news, Mr. Greyson, is you fell asleep during their visit and didn't wake up. You died yesterday afternoon." Pete reaches to grab a dining chair, swings it over next to the bed and sits on it.

My brain empties; then fills with resentment. "That's not much of a joke. I don't appreciate your humor." I respond as coldly as I can. Why would he say such a thing?

Pete leans forward in the chair. "Mr. Greyson, this is no joke. I'm sorry to give you the news; dying is the bad news. The good news is you're in Heaven."

"I'm really dead?" I struggle to breathe. Need air.

"Yes, sir."

"In Heaven." Can't feel my arms, my legs.

"Yes."

My mind swirls. Spinning faster and faster. A whirlwind in my head. I can't grab a thought. Nothing in my head. Everything vanished. Pete is sitting there, looking at me. I don't know who me is. "This is Heaven."

"Yes, part of it," Pete says. I hear the words but they mean nothing.

Slow deep breathes. Concentrate. "I'm dead." That's

4

all I can say; my only thought. Dead, dead, dead, and it's pounding in my head.

"Yes. Surprisingly, you can tell you're dead by how good you feel." He smiles. "Kind of counter-intuitive, wouldn't you say?"

Think. Must think. A person doesn't die every day. Slow down, take your time. I feel great, so I have to be dead. Can't beat that logic. I'm dead. Oh gosh! I died yesterday. Yesterday I died. Today I'm dead. Today I'm in Heaven. Can't be. Can't be. This is bad, really bad. Somebody made a huge mistake. What am I going to do? Take it easy. At least my brain works again. Have to say something, but I hate what I must do. I sigh, a big, end-it-all-now sigh. May as well get the worst bad news over with.

"Pete, I'm an atheist. I don't believe in Heaven and I don't believe in God."

"Yes, we know."

"You know."

"Yup."

Pete's tone is that of a New Englander being asked if he knows the way into town. Almost an "ayup." Casual; no sense of awe or even concern. And I'm dead, dead, dead, dead, and dead. And in Heaven. This is a Mad Hatter's tea party.

I died yesterday. At this moment I am dead and lying in a bed in Heaven. Okay. Strange, weird, uncomfortable, hard to understand, but I'm breathing and I'm thinking. I was sick, very sick and I died. What I knew was going to happen someday, happened yesterday. Can't complain my time finally came. Sooner than I wanted, but okay. Wasn't bad. Falling asleep and dying, couldn't ask for a much better death. What about Beth and the kids, and the grand-kids? How are they? I sit higher in the bed, something I hadn't done in a while.

"My family?"

"They're doing fine. You went to sleep as you some-times did, but you slept longer than usual and your breath-ing became labored. Your family called in a doctor who checked, listening to your lungs and your heart. She stood after leaning over you and told your family you were dy-ing. They were shocked at first. Over the next few minutes, discussing possibilities and options with the doc-tor, they accepted the situation and agreed there would be no extraordinary efforts to resuscitate you. Your death was understood, they were prepared. It was gentle."

They must be sad. Why don't I feel sad for them? Why don't I feel sad for myself?

"Why don't I feel sad?"

"Ah, yes. The concept of death from your side, the side of the living. Death is laying down heavy burdens, isn't it? Rest for weary bones. Parting from loved ones. Never again playing with grandchildren. The end to lazy summer afternoons sitting in a boat in the middle of a lake casting for dinner when you don't really care about catch-ing anything. Yes, the joys of life. And for atheists like you, the end of all possibilities and the folding of con-sciousness into nothingness. Death, the most profound loss for the living. But, hey, from this side, the side of the afterlife and Heaven lies an infinity of possibilities and more love than you could ever imagine. Pete spread his arms out wide. "You don't need to be sad. Nothing to be sad about. You know it. You can feel it."

Okay. I'm a guy; not a manly man with a five o'clock shadow by lunchtime, but a guy. Feelings are not where I live. But death. That's a big deal; gotta have feelings about being dead, especially for those I left. I search inside. Don't find feelings. Not quite right. I'm fabulously content. Anything else? Curious. More? Content, curious, and something more. Confused. The three Cs of death, contentment, curiosity, and confusion. A touch of anxiety? Not sure. Back to the issue at hand; the deal breaker. I always tried to look for the bright side; there isn't one here. But I have to tell the truth.

"I'm an atheist, Pete. That has to mean something."

I hope my thin voice doesn't betray my fear. In a heartbeat I might slip and slide into a fate that couldn't be possible. Hell was never a consideration and now it could be real and I might soon stand at the gates of it.

"And you're concerned you're in the wrong place. By the way, may I call you Mike?"

"Of course. And, yes, I'm concerned. I didn't believe there was an afterlife, but here I am. I was wrong. When you don't have faith, I understand you go someplace else." I made a terrible mistake and I'm going to pay for it. Here it comes. Stomach churning; almost fainting. Brace yourself.

"There is no someplace else."

Confused, but relieved. Let's review. I died yesterday. I'm dead and in Heaven. I've just learned there is no Hell by someone who should know and at the moment I'm not keen on asking any more questions about faith. I'm not worried about my family. My major emotion is contentment, which seems reasonable. Pete is a director of sorts for the good and bad. And I'm breathing normally.

"Pete, what is your job?"

"To be your guide for the first week or two, until you get your bearings. There is a lot to learn. I'm here to help. Why don't I make coffee while we chat?" Pete walks into the kitchenette while I continue to make sense of what and where I am.

"Are you dead too?"

Pete answers while facing away spooning coffee into the filter. "No. I'm like you, except I never lived on earth, or anywhere else."

"What am I? A ghost, a spirit, an angel?"

"You're not really a what; you're more of a where. You're in Heaven, same as me. The only difference is I am here to guide you. It will all make good sense in time."

I hear coffee dripping into the pot and revel in the familiar aroma. Pete returns to sit next to the bed. I'm an atheist; at least I was when I was alive. Now I'm in Heaven. That means God exists. Pete could be an angel. But I have another question.

"How did I die, what killed me? I was sure I would be going home."

"Your congestive heart failure finally overwhelmed your body. Your lungs couldn't provide enough oxygen. And you hadn't been eating which further weakened your body. Everything just wore out at the same time. Nothing could have been done, except keep you artificially alive in the critical care unit. You'd be on a respirator for a few days or weeks, semiconscious and uncomfortable, but so-called alive. Your family made a merciful decision. May I ask you a question?"

"Sure."

"Were you prepared?"

"To die?"

"Yes." Pete rises at the beep of the coffeemaker and returns to the counter.

I expected death would be the end of me. One day I would cease to exist, be the same as I was before the egg and sperm fell in love, nothing.

"All I did was accept the reality of no afterlife and keep a grip on my composure. I wanted to die well for my family, ease their grief and fear. I hope I did a good job of it. Can you tell me if it worked?"

Pete answers as he pours the coffee. "Yes, I can confirm you did a good job. Your family was comforted by your attitude, by your acceptance and, I must say, how much you expressed your love for them and how you embraced their love for you."

Pete returns with two cups of coffee and hands me one; black, as I like it.

"Your name...Pete. That's not like Saint Peter, reviewing my life for entrance at the Pearly Gates?"

"Nope. If there were gates, you're past them."

"I didn't see a bright white light."

Pete's hands cover his mouth; eyes wide open.

"You didn't? Oh no. No white light you say?"

"What?" Heart pounding again.

Why did I bring that up? I was feeling good; I was just kidding around. What did I know? Could be bad people just die; good people see a white light and move toward Heaven. What have I done?

Pete lowers his hands and leans back in his chair.

"The bright light some people say they see when they are clinically dead is simply brain neurons firing. Means nothing, especially since none of them die, at least not then. Trust me; this is where you are meant to be."

Relief. Now I understand the need of a guide like Pete, although a more solemn tone would be nice. Being dead is not easy. Well, it's easy to be dead, but strange to be dead yet know you're dead. And to be in Heaven. Sounds good but discombobulatingly odd.

Pete continues. "Why don't you get up, shower and get dressed? You'll find clothes in the closet and I'll make us breakfast."

I do just that. Up, shower, shave, which seems strange to do in Heaven, dress, and sit at the table facing scrambled eggs, bacon, hash browns and sourdough toast; with orange juice and more coffee. Looks wonderful. Smells fantastic. Tastes out of this world.

We discuss my situation for an hour or so, when Pete makes a suggestion. If I want, I can go out the door and be at the trailhead of one of my favorite day hikes, to Lake 22. Give yourself a chance to relax and ground yourself in a favorite activity and mull things over, he says. Should take into late afternoon. We can meet back here for dinner and wrap up the first day in Heaven. He shoves a daypack into my hands. "I packed what you will need."

When I open the door, the parking area at the trailhead for the hike to Lake 22 waits. It's empty. Over on the left is my usual parking spot, far enough from the trailhead to avoid bumps and scratches from wide backpacks and clumsy hikers and far enough from the trees to avoid bird droppings. Small birds in the nearby trees like to perch on car side view mirrors. They sit there long enough to leave presents. I learned the hard way those small birds discharge a lot of poop. The dirt and stones and sand under my boots are the sensations of home. My deteriorating health ended my hikes to Lake 22 about ten years earlier. Lake 22 isn't its official name. My friend Rudy loves this route so much he said if you hike it once, you'll hike to the lake at least twenty-two times in your life; so that's what we called it.

Just before stepping on the trail, I glance back at the door, half-expecting to see nothing, or a Dali-esque door hanging in space in the middle of nowhere. But there is the door, the front of a building, whitewashed adobe, one story, about eight hundred square feet. Normal enough, under the circumstances. I laugh at myself. What would I know about normal under the circumstances? Nothing, that's what.

I start the trail. It is eight miles to the lake, up and down hills with an elevation gain of almost two thousand feet. The path twists through thick forests of cedar and pine. The last part near the lake would be above the tree line, mostly boulders, scree, grass, moss, and a few bushes.

After two hours of sheer delight, huffing up slopes, smelling the forest, gazing at the sky, and otherwise forgetting I was dead, I reach Whisper Rock, my name for the last place for cell phone coverage and where I phone Beth to tell her how I am doing. I call it Whisper Rock because when I was on the phone I sure didn't want to disturb other hikers who also wanted to enjoy the wilderness. Out of habit, I suppose, I reach for my left front pocket and of course, no phone. There is no one to call. Yet again, no sadness. Are only selected feelings allowed in Heaven? Seems like a good idea and intrusive at the same time. I relax on the rock to ponder my situation. I suppose this is why Pete suggested the hike, to reflect on being dead. The sun moderates a chill wind as I lean on the rock. I am dead. I am in Heaven, part of it as Pete said, the orientation part, I guess. Orientation to being dead after arriving in Heaven seems reasonable. No more thoughts arise. I reach into the pack and pull out two granola bars. They're the same green wrapped ones I enjoyed in the old days. Where would they get granola bars in Heaven? Is there a factory somewhere? And what about breakfast? Are there egg laying chickens in Heaven? Do they slaughter pigs for bacon in Heaven? Who made the hash browns? The chill wind carries away the sun's warmth. I stand, pull on the daypack and start up the next hill.

Muscles ache by the time I reach Lake 22. I find my favorite viewing spot among three boulders and look over the scene before me. The lake is about a hundred feet below, almost round, and reflects the clouds from its surface. I smile. My first thought is, "I could stay here forever." Right. Next set of thoughts. What is real? This obviously is not the real Lake 22 trail; it's a beautiful day yet the trail is empty. The granola bars were not real granola bars. How would Heaven import granola bars? Why did I even eat? Sheltered from the wind, the sun is warm, a short nap sounds good. Do I even need to sleep? I should compile of list of questions to ask Pete.

The issues; what are the issues of being dead? Dead isn't the state of nothingness I had assumed. Had I known this, I wonder if I would have taken more chances when I was alive. I wanted to jump out of a plane; never did. I considered running for Superintendent of Schools; didn't do that either. It seemed clear to me too, that I was a member of the impulsive, immature, clown half of the species. Was my fate sealed at birth? Did I win in life; did I lose; does it matter? How should I have kept score? A more interesting life might have been an exhausting one, stretching myself to the limit or even a dangerous one earning a well-deserved rest in the hereafter. Seems like I wasted my life not doing what I could have. How much was my life avoiding what I feared? Enough wondering. I have to turn off my mind for a moment and sooth my soul by feeding my body.

A quick search of the daypack secures a tuna sandwich on whole wheat, my standard daytrip lunch. Nestled in between the rocks, enjoying the sweetest tuna sandwich ever, I ponder more. Nothing I can do about being dead. Heaven seems like a nice place. I'm experiencing mostly positive emotions. There must be a reason an atheist is allowed in Heaven. There might be degrees of Heaven. It could be my experience of Heaven won't be a lot of fun. Must be a good reason it takes a week or two to figure things out. Another search of the pack brings out a plastic storage bag of chocolate chip cookies, my favorite. Homemade. Warm. In Heaven cookies are warm!

I sit looking at the lake and pondering for a good hour, hesitant to leave a familiar place to face my surprise chance at eternity. The quality of Heaven might depend on what I figure out.

In my early twenties, starting out in life, sometimes I would suddenly wake in the middle of the night, terrorized, fearing death will gut my life before I even have one. The dread of inevitability, of powerlessness, of helpless panic was overwhelming. With marriage and children and a developing career that panic faded. I was creating a history, a life of meaning, fulfilling responsibilities, experiencing the phases of living and the joys and sorrows of graying hair and diminishing abilities. Did I do it right?

What defines a good life? My idea was my life had to be my life, no one else's. God wouldn't want me to waste my unique existence being like everyone else. What would be the point of that? And if God did not exist, why would I want me to be like everyone else anyway? I was certain when alive that I was the sole maker and judger of my existence. All life has worth, but not all lives have value. How does a person determine the value of his or her life; or any life? I thought I knew. Now I'm not so sure, not sure at all. What have I fallen into?

Back on the trail, descending toward home. Love. Did Beth know how much I loved her? I could have shown her more deeply and more often. Same with the kids. The grandkids were easy. I told them all the time.

Whoa. I must have missed it on the hike up, a tiny yellow flower growing in the middle of the trail and I almost stepped on it. You can't step on a flower in Heaven; has to be a rule against it. Springtime. Should always be spring in Heaven. The trail is dry, not the mud that it usually was in spring. Don't know how many times I slipped in the mud and landed on my keister. This little guy is proudly in the middle of things saying "Here I am." In the summer all the plants are fully-grown and glorious, adding to the splendor of the outdoors. When the wind shifts and comes from the north, branches become dry and brittle, leaves turn brown, fall off, and are pushed along the ground by the wind. In winter most plants will be covered by snow and many will be gone. People my age will say, "It all goes so quickly." It did for me and I'm in Heaven. Now what will become of me? What's after winter?

The hike down the mountain takes much less time than the way up, but I still arrive at the trailhead and the building at dusk, later than I anticipated. I am sore in every muscle, bone, ligament, and tendon, loving every ache. The mild discomfort is invigorating compared to the unhappy maladies that had become my daily life. There is no pain, only physical awareness. Out of breath is from activity, not lungs that no longer work.

I smell sizzling steaks as soon as I open the door. Pete exchanges my daypack for a glass of pinot noir. After dinner, Pete and I sit to talk more about life and death.

"I know I'm dead. I accept that."

"Good."

"Why aren't I unhappy about it?"

"What would be the point?"

What would be the point? Good question. If I were dead as I expected to be, I would not exist. I would experience no feelings, sadness or any other. If I die and end up in Heaven, why would I be sad? I would have been sad to end in Hell, but that doesn't seem to be the case—or is it?

Oh no. Ohhh no. Breath catching. An old Twilight Zone TV episode leaps into my mind, about a crook killed as he tried to escape the police. He ended up in a luxury apartment, not unlike my current room, with a guide just like Pete! The crook was given anything he wanted and what he wanted was wine, women, and lots of money. All of it was his, anything and everything. After a month he was bored, said he didn't like Heaven and wanted to go to the other place. His guide said with a smug smile, "Why do you think you're in Heaven?" Could that be me? I must face the music one more time.

"Pete, I'm not sure if you're aware of this kind of thing, but there was a Twilight Zone episode on television, must be from the early sixties about a crook who died and thought he went to Heaven..."

"Yeah, I'm familiar with the story. Title was 'Nice Place to Visit.'"

"Is that...?"

Pete smiles that nice smile of his, warm, caring, almost angelic, "No. That is not your situation. Heaven is a good place. No one is tormented for eternity; no point to that. No lessons to learn, no punishment for evil deeds. No nothingness for nonbelievers."

"Okay. That was a worry, as much as I can seem to worry. Everything is more from curiosity. Speaking of which, you mentioned I'm more a where than a what. Can you explain? And what or where are you?"

"You're also wondering what is real?"

"That was on my list."

"Let's start there, with what is real. How about an after dinner Scotch?"

I nod. Wine and Scotch in Heaven. Who would have imagined that?

Pete goes to a cupboard in the kitchen, pulls out a bottle of Red Label, to another cupboard for two glasses, fills the glasses with ice from the dispenser in the refrigerator door and returns to pour each of us a drink.

"Is this from Scotland?"

"Ah yes," he smiles. "Is it real? Mike, where you are now, everything is real, including the Scotch."

"Where does everything come from?"

Pete purses his lips. "It doesn't come from anywhere. It is where it needs to be when it needs to be there. I am here because I need to be here. You are here because you need to be here. The trail to Lake 22 was there because it needed to be there. This room is here because it needs to be here."

I'm a pretty smart guy, Masters in Education from Stanford. I understand the words; have no idea what Pete means.

"Sounds like magic."

"Not magic, physics."

I sip on the Scotch to take a momentary mental break. The ice against my lips settles me down, a little.

"Physics."

"Yes, let me explain. Everything, all energy and all matter, stars, people, marshmallows, x-rays, contain information. If you decode that information and then encode it, you can decode it again, whenever and wherever you want. Take the egg and sperm. Tiny, tiny things, containing the information to create a fully functioning adult human being. Just decode the information in the DNA and do what it says. Similarly, a strip of fried bacon, if you decode the information, has all the information needed to create a sizzling slice of bacon, without creating a pig, raising it, slaughtering it, curing the meat and finally frying it. Encode and decode, and you can create ready to eat bacon. Everything, and I mean everything, contains the information needed to make it again."

I'm getting it. One question will tell.

"What about emotions and thoughts?"

"Emotions and thoughts, both are matter, such as brain cells and neurotransmitters and both are energy, such as electrical impulses and are encoded in the brain cells by how and where cells are connected and what the ratios of various neurochemicals are. And as you know, matter and energy can convert into each other."

"I am here because I was encoded while alive and then decoded after I died?"

"Very good."

"What about you? Where did you come from?"

"I was decoded because you needed me to be decoded."

"You're a figment of my imagination?"

"Not at all. I'm real, decoded information just like you are." Pete takes a drink of his Scotch, although I doubt he needs it. I need it and take a healthy sip.

"Who or what does the encoding and decoding?"

"Ah," Pete smiles. "That is the big question. The question of all questions. I suggest you sleep on it."

"We're talking about God, aren't we?"

"Yes. Which is why I suggest we take a look at what everything means tomorrow after breakfast. There is a lot to discuss about God and we should do it all in one go."

"Sounds good. What happens to you now?

"I disappear, watch."

He stands, walks to the front door, opens it, waves goodbye, and closes the door behind him. Just like a normal person.

There are pajamas lying on the end of the bed. I leave my clothes on the nearby chair and follow my nighttime routine, including brushing my teeth, all the while questioning why I should brush my teeth.

After climbing under the covers, I wonder if I'll get much sleep with all the thoughts roiling in my head. But I am content. Not a bad condition for someone who is dead.

Day
2

God, Einstein and Everything

Oh boy. I'm awake. Eyes closed. Was it a dream? If I open my eyes will I be in my hospital room? Do I want to be in my hospital room, alive, sick, dying? Or do I prefer already being dead? There is a gentle knock on the door. I open my eyes. I'm not in a hospital room. I'm in my new room. I'm still dead.

"Come in."

"Good morning, Mike." Pete walks through the door dressed much like yesterday except with a yellow shirt. I didn't notice before how tall he is; a college basketball player twenty-five pounds past his playing days.

"Hi, Pete. Good to see you. I wasn't sure about opening my eyes and finding out I wasn't dead."

"Takes getting used to. Why don't we follow yesterday's routine? You get up and dressed, I'll make breakfast. What would you like?"

"Can you do a sausage and cheese omelet?"

"I trust that has been encoded. And juice, coffee?"

"Apple, and black coffee like yesterday, please. No toast."

I pounce as soon as we clear the dishes from the table and relax in the living area with final cups of coffee.

"God."

"What would you like to know?"

"First, if you've been encoded because of me, how do you know anything more than I do? How would you know things I don't know?"

"Simple. You've been decoded as you from the information encoded during your life. I've been decoded with information encoded from many other sources. It's as if you're in first grade and I'm a college professor. No offense."

"None taken. I feel like I'm in first grade. I'm a See Dick Run schoolbook and you're a set of encyclopedias."

"Yes." Pete imperially bows from the waist.

"Back to God. Is there a God?"

"Yes and no."

That answer mirrored much of my adult life, beginning around twenty when I declared myself an agnostic. By age forty, I decided agnostics were wimp atheists too afraid to admit God didn't exist so I declared myself a born-again atheist. However, now I am dead, in Heaven, lounging in a chair, drinking a cup of what is probably Kona coffee, perhaps I should rethink my position.

"Go on."

Pete takes a sip of his coffee and places the cup on the table, ready for his discourse. I do the same with my cup, ready to listen. What I grasp could make the difference between Heaven and nothingness.

"To understand God, we first must understand life. Let's start at the bottom and work up. Plants and animals are both alive. Is there any difference in the life of a plant and an animal? Not really, details are different, but both are alive and then they die. The first issue is: what is life? Second, humans and other higher life forms exhibit degrees of self-awareness. Humans seem to have the highest level. The significance of self-awareness is issue number two. Third is: what being, if any, made life happen? Fourth and last is: is there a purpose to this life thing? Other issues and uncertainties complicate matters, but these four are sufficient to understand God. Questions?"

"Keep going." So far, so good. My brain is in full operational readiness. I'm content and curious; not confused, not anxious.

"More coffee?" Pete stands and heads to the kitchen.

"Yes, please." A jolt of caffeine wouldn't hurt. Coffee in Heaven, who knew?

Pete continues from the kitchen as he reaches for the pot. "Okay. First order of business is to decide if life is significant compared to nonlife. In other words, is a deer more important than a rock? The answer is no. Living things are nonessential to the workings of the universe."

"That's harsh. Are you including humans?"

"Yes. At this point." Pete returns with the pot and pours us each a cup. I take a moment to put my nose to the coffee and inhale the dark aroma before leaning back in the chair as he sits and continues. Contentment is percolating from my pores, but I must keep my focus.

"As for self-awareness, not much there either. The

universe doesn't need it and such consciousness only causes trouble; mostly with our awareness of mortality, which, ironically, leads people into bigotry, conflicts, wars and murder. Many postulate that the knowledge of death gave rise to the invention of gods. But that's not the issue. People can invent anything they want, automobiles, type-writers, even gods, but that has nothing to do with a real god. If you examine cultural histories, people created gods to account for events going on around them including darkness and light, rain, the seasons, life and death. What made sense for ancient people were gods with human traits and human interests. Gods changed as cultures changed. A real god wouldn't change, only the way we define a god changes. Which gets us to issue number three: who, if anything, created all this? Ready?"

Deep breath. "Ready."

"All right. Accept that people created gods the best way they could conceptualize, which were as super people. These gods were not true gods, just people inventions. If there was a real god in charge of everything in the universe, it would be unlikely that God was human-like. Why pick a lifeform from a minor planet in a minor solar system in a minor galaxy among billions and billions of others?"

"What about God making man in His own image?"

"That's what people said because that's the best way they could make sense. What else could they say; god was a multi-gender mutant from the planet Zoltar? Or maybe a Puerto Rican bathhouse attendant with a magic machine to control the world? The point I want to make is that if God exists, it is doubtful God is a humanoid type being. But, something had to create us and all that is around us. We can say God did, and be right, depending on how we define God. Can you accept that as a working hypothesis?"

"Okay." I believe Pete could talk all day, and if so, I will listen all day.

"That last issue is: was the universe and all that is in it, including people, made for a purpose. The answer is no. The universe and everything in it just is."

"I want to argue that one. If I'm in Heaven, life and death must have meaning. Meaning depends on someone, and I'm totally willing at the moment to consider God probably, making judgements. My life, my death, one way or another, had to have meaning." I take a sip of coffee and continue with as much confidence as I can muster. "How can you be sure there isn't a purpose to existence, human or otherwise, but especially human?"

"What would be the purpose?"

"You're the encyclopedia. You must have ideas that great people entertain."

"I'll tell you what. I'll introduce you to a friend of mine who can explain the reality of the universe and we can go on from there. Want to meet one of the true greats?"

"Absolutely." I don't know why I am so confident, but I am and it feels good.

"Super. Outside next to the pool are two lounge chairs. Go sit in one and I'll send him over."

I had no idea we had a pool, but I open the door and there it is, nearer than the trailhead of yesterday, but no less surprising. Two aluminum lounge chairs with green plastic webbing sit on the pool deck separated by a cheap plastic table with a clear top. I sit in the left one facing more away from the door. The form of an old man ambles toward me; instantly recognizable with his wild hair and eyebrows and with a moustache attached to a mischievous grin. Albert Einstein is about to sit next to me. I stand and hold out my hand. He shakes it and says with a trace of an accent, "Hello, I am Professor Einstein. How do you do?"

"Pleasure to meet you, Professor. My name is Mike. Please have a seat."

We sit and swing our legs onto the chairs. On the table between us are now two glasses of iced tea with straws, the bendy kind.

"You have questions?"

"Yes." I gesture with my arms to encompass everything around us. "What is all this about?"

"Let us examine what was and what is."

Albert and I, our two chairs, the table and two glasses of iced tea are transported to nowhere. As he describes it, no where and no when.

"We are sitting together to watch the big bang, the beginning of everything," he says. "There is nothing here, no space and no time. Do you notice anything?"

"Just us."

"Exactly. Now watch where I'm pointing. Everything you see will be in ultra-super slow motion. One millisecond of real time, once time starts, will take ten minutes our time. We are looking at the beginning of everything we know. Keep in mind, right now there is no matter, no space and no time. Nothing exists in the universe because there is no universe. Watch, here it comes."

I expect an explosion, blinding light, deafening noise and a shock wave powerful enough to send us and our chairs tumbling into deep space. Instead, something invisible gets bigger. That's the best way I can describe it. No noise. No light. It is a shadow, but not dark, and gets larger, the size of our sun in a millisecond, our time.

"First it expands, and then inflation starts, growing faster than the speed of light. Cooling begins and the laws of physics are born, along with matter and antimatter. Keep in mind the big bang was not an expansion into the universe. The expansion *is* the universe; it grew the universe like the inside of a balloon inflates.

Over the next ten minutes, Albert describes what is happening, talking so fast he almost runs out of breath. Then he speeds up time to enable us to observe more events.

"Gravity just separated from the other forces. Here's the strong nuclear force and some particles have mass. And now the universe has cooled to only a trillion degrees." Albert shakes his head. "Do you understand that? Cooled to a trillion degrees! Over the next 250,000 years or so, the universe will cool off enough so various types of matter can exist. Here is what it looks like."

Nothing changes. It is still dark, the shadowy thing all around us, but I see nothing I can define.

"Here it is after about 400 million years."

Stars have formed. The universe is finally visible. But it isn't much.

"A few stars, but mostly radiation. Gravity and electro-magnetism will soon accelerate the development of stars and the universe becomes what it is in our time." Albert takes a sip of his iced tea. "Questions?"

"How old is the universe?"

"About 14.7 billion years." He emphasizes point seven, excited by the precision, I think.

"Any uncertainty to that?"

"No. It is not an alternative fact, a fake-fact, a question, an assumption or a hypothesis. It is fact."

"How about life? How old?"

"On earth about three and a half billion years. Older in other places."

"Interesting."

"Interesting?" His eyes widen in wonder. "Extraordinarily fantastic. Life has to be the most remarkable event in the universe. How did it happen? Where did it happen? The answers are also fantastic; life began in the stars. Water, that necessary ingredient to life as we know it, depended on supernovas exploding, creating oxygen and throwing it into the void. Water, all water on earth arrived via asteroids and comets. Our immense oceans filled one bucket at a time, as it were. Primitive life too, probably arrived the same way." The professor paused, then continued.

"Seems like a miracle that in the vastness of space, these gifts arrived on our small planet. But the universe has a secret, the secret of time, enough time to enable many things to happen, and happen more than once. Given an infinity of time, anything is possible, including life.

"Speaking of life, also interesting is death, the periods of mass extinctions of life on earth. 440 million years ago, 86% of all species died. 251 million years ago we lost

96% of all species. The dinosaurs and a total of 76% of species were lost only 66 million years ago. Species come and go," he sighed. "But mostly go. Humans could be one of them to go."

"Makes you wonder about the meaning of life."

"That it does. But let's explore more of the universe."

We sail our chairs and table and iced teas to view a giant nebula of green, pink, gold and blue; a cloud of dust, hydrogen, helium, and plasma and majestic beauty and the place where stars are born. One in the distance looks like a seahorse. I ask Albert if we can sail our chairs through the cloud and he shakes his head. "For one thing," he says, "with so little matter, there is nothing to go through. For another thing, this nebula is about fifteen light years across and three hundred light years away."

We hop on a comet. Albert and I place our chairs on the hard rock and ice surface and sit facing forward. Albert takes his pipe out of a pocket, stuffs in tobacco and lights it. We sit for a while with nothing happening except him puffing away so I ask a question. "How soon is it going to move?" Albert almost chokes. He puts his pipe on the table and turns toward me.

"Our current velocity is about four-hundred thousand miles per hour," he says, but in a vacuum, no air resistance." Albert also explains how vast space is, and thus how empty no matter how large things are. Physicists measure distance in light years, almost six trillion miles. It could be weeks, months, even years before we are close enough to another object to note our relative speed. Mere mortals measure distance by how many minutes to the next gas station or burger joint. We're sitting on a comet going almost half a million miles an hour and nary a hair on his head is ruffled. But with his wild hair it would be hard to tell anyway. This is so cool.

We speed alongside meteors and asteroids, buzzing the planets of our own solar system and take a long-range look at a dozen galaxies.

"Do you comprehend all this?" I ask.

He nodded. "I do."

"Can we talk about it?"

We touch down back at poolside, fresh iced teas on the table.

"What would you like to talk about?"

"What does it mean? All that we saw, the immensity of space, energy turning into matter, the beginning, how much can the universe expand and what happens at the end?"

"There was nothing until the universe began and then the laws of physics came into being. The universe will expand for eternity, until it becomes an empty cold place. 'What does it mean?' It means nothing." He sips his iced tea as if he just said the bus was late rather than what he did, that life has no meaning.

"What about Heaven? Aren't we in Heaven?"

"Yes, Heaven. Let me explain. A current theory in physics is string theory. It attempts to unify gravity and particle physics to help us create a theory of everything; a task I worked on for years. Various models of that theory postulate extra dimensions of space-time. Bosonic string theory for example has twenty-six dimensions while the supergravity theory has eleven. These are mathematical constructs and in theory only; there is still a lot to learn. I don't expect you to understand the math, but I hope you can accept the possibilities of dimensions beyond the three you are familiar with, height, width, and depth, and, of course, the fourth, time. You don't have to understand what they are like, but can you entertain more than four dimensions?"

"Yes." I think I understood one word for every ten he spoke. Being tutored by Albert Einstein is not easy.

"Good, because now I want to explain Heaven. The string theorists are correct to propose additional dimensions. However, their math and theory are woefully inadequate. There are over eleven-thousand dimensions—11,587 to be exact."

At this, my brain fries and my eyes glaze over. Albert doesn't notice. "Eleven-thousand dimensions."

"Yes. If you listed them in order of increasing complexity, earth's three dimensions would be seven, nine and fourteen. You can appreciate the potential of the other dimensions, most notably combinations of dimensions. This enables Heaven to exist. Heaven is the combination of 7691 dimensions, including the most complicated. I understand that Pete has explained encoding and decoding. Imagine the power of these dimensions to encode everything and decode it as needed. Perhaps this is what people consider to be God."

"That sounds like a computer, decoding and encoding, processing information."

"Perhaps."

"What's your opinion?" I'm straining to keep up. I must understand what he is telling me.

"My opinion is if God exists, this God exists through

the beauty and structure of the universe. There is no God living in the sky worrying about me and whether I am a good man or a bad one. Perhaps this Heaven we find ourselves in supports that position."

"What about good and evil?"

"A person can be good or evil without the oversight of a God. In fact, it was Shakespeare who said something like, 'nothing is either good or bad but thinking makes it so.' Good and bad is our job, not God's."

I'm exhausted. Pete said it would take a week or two to get situated and now I understand why. I had to fit in somehow and what I learned today supports my position on God, sort of: At least that God isn't watching over us from a home in the sky. I push myself out of the chair and stand next to one of the greatest minds in history and hold out my hand. Albert rises and we shake hands.

"Professor, this has been one of the best days of my life." I pause at the absurdity of what I just said. "Professor, let me restart. Thank you for this enlightening experience."

"You are welcome," he says, as if this were just a normal day. With that, he turns and walks back in the same direction he had come until he is out of sight. I collapse in the chair.

Heaven is multiple dimensions. God might exist but probably not in the God-is-like-a-human sense. God, if one or more exists, may not be concerned about our individual lives. With that definition, Heaven isn't a reward from God for worshiping Him. Heaven exists because all those dimensions exist. That would make sense for my being here. And make sense of why bad things happen to good people. Feels flat though. A deer and a rock are equal? Equally accidental and equally useless? Then why should human life continue in Heaven if life has no meaning, including, especially, human life? Confusion has returned; accompanied by a serving of anxiety.

Time to go inside. I open the door.

"Hi, Mike, welcome back. I hope you're hungry. Just for fun I sent out for pizza, one veggi and one meat lovers. We have that and a plus-size bottle of chardonnay."

"You sent out for pizza. I still don't understand this place."

"How was your day with Professor Einstein?"

"Ever seen the inside of a star?"

Pete shakes his head. "Can't say I have."

"I've looked into the interior of a star and eye-to-eye with a beam of light, and observed space from the inside of a black hole. It was a good day."

"You know, between you, me and the lamppost, the professor behaves as if the universe is his. Not that he owns it, but that he knows the most about it. He loves showing it off. Did you learn anything important to you?" Pete sets out plates, knives and forks, napkins, two boxes of Domino's pizza, two wine glasses and what looks like a half-gallon bottle of white wine. I pour the wine.

"Yes, but I'm not sure what is really important."

"That's why I'm here."

"Good. My understanding, at the moment, is Heaven and God are multiple dimensions I've never heard about. Einstein seems content that God is in the structure of the universe and doesn't create or control individual humans or humans as a group as far as I can understand."

"Doesn't that mesh with your ideas?"

"Pretty much, except the thousands of dimensions; had no idea that was coming. I'm in Heaven because Heaven exists, not that I did anything deserving to get in. I like an all accepting afterlife, but I wonder what happens to the bad guys. There should be consequences. And I'm not comfortable with God being reduced to information processing."

"But God doesn't exist for you."

I reach for a second piece of meat lovers.

"Now I'm here, I'd like Heaven to be more meaningful and personal, like I achieved something important. This feels like hopping on the next bus that comes along; that life was only a preamble to get here, that everybody gets here and I haven't figured out what here is, or why here is."

"You want life to have meaning and a God to decide what is good and what isn't? I thought you already had that conversation with yourself."

"That was before. Now I know Heaven exists, I have to understand what that means."

I'm sure my head is spinning. I notice Pete is finishing his fourth piece of pizza; no wonder the young fellow is developing a gut.

"Heaven 'just is' doesn't cut it?" he says, reaching for yet another piece of pizza.

"Not yet." How can there be eleven-thousand dimensions?

"Well, here's a thought. Did Professor Einstein explain the dimensions to you?"

"He said I didn't have to understand the math, but I get the idea."

"The math might be important."

I shake my head. "The math is way over my head."

"No, it isn't. All you to do is subtract."

"Explain."

"There are 11,587 total dimensions, right?"

"So I'm told." I'm pretending to understand how this could be so.

"Heaven comprises 7,691 of them, right?"

"Right."

"Heaven has 7,691 dimensions and therefore the rest of the universe has only 3,896. What this means to me is that Heaven is more complex than the rest of the universe; almost twice as much and that doesn't include how complicated the higher dimensions are. Heaven is more powerful. And dare I say, more God-like than the regular universe?"

I'm speechless. Simple math defining God? I'm still fixed on that bible passage that we are made in His image. It is discomforting even for an atheist to imagine God properties in a collection of dimensions. God should not be machine-like or merely information collecting, encoding and decoding. If God exists, God should be...what? I don't know.

I grab a third piece of pizza, this time the veggi, and pour more wine into our two glasses.

"Pete, I'm confused, overwhelmed and to be frank, a bit anxious. This adjusting to being dead and landing in Heaven and eleven-thousand dimensions and traveling in space with Einstein is hard to get my head around.

"Sounds like a good stopping point for today. Why don't I clean up the dishes, take my leave and we can start again tomorrow?"

"I can do the dishes."

Pete gets up. "All right," and walks to the door. "Oh, by the way, do you realize you cannot see, hear or touch the multiple dimensions any more than you can see, hear or touch God?" Pete shrugs his shoulders. "Just being the Devil's Advocate. Catch you tomorrow," and off he goes.

When the door clicks shut, a chill runs through me. Oh gosh, why did he say Devil's Advocate? Some sort of hint? Is he a real Devil's advocate? We'll start again tomorrow, he said.

Big sigh. Mellow out. Don't worry. You've got a lot to learn yet. Relax, relax. Let contentment drift to the surface and fears sink to the bottom. Contentment filling my body. Be in the moment. Look around. Be happy.

Dinner is yet to be cleared. I'm still not sure of Pete's job description, but I can clean up after myself. Before I do, though, I pour myself a Scotch on the rocks and relax on the couch. What is this place? The bed was made. Did Pete do that? Did God do that? Did one or more dimensions do that? No phone. No television. No radio or CD player. Who would I call, what would be on television? No windows. Is the door locked? If it's locked, am I locked in, a prisoner? Why would there be locks in Heaven? I get up and try the door. No lock. It opens, revealing the pool and two chairs, and a table without drinks. Past the pool is a flat darkness, back dropped by a silhouette of mountains and the pink afterglow of sunset. What you might see in

Arizona or New Mexico.

Back on the couch, I continue my inspection. No clocks, not even on the stove or microwave oven. There is the couch I am sitting on and two matching chairs and the coffee table. A coffeemaker and blender sit next to the sink on the counter. I don't see a place for a washer or dryer and no place for a water heater or furnace. There is a dishwasher. Something every home should have, even in Heaven.

As I put the leftovers into the refrigerator and everything cleanable into the dishwasher, I realize I had missed lunch, but hadn't been hungry until Pete mentioned dinner. Do we have to eat here? I think about the need for toilet paper and what happens to my clothes. I put them on the chair when I took them off. They weren't there in the morning. Did Pete do something with my clothes while I showered? There were always clothes hanging in the closet. I'll have to ask him.

What a day. Spent most of it soaring through the universe with Albert Einstein and now I'm wondering what happens to my underwear. I pour myself another Scotch and return to the couch. Time for a self-assessment. Quick check, still feeling the three Cs of death: contentment, curiosity and confusion. Two days in. That's progress. Toward a forever that means everything, but I don't yet understand what it is and why I am part of it. Something is missing.

Day
3

Old Folks, New World

I'm lying on my stomach, just awake. Since being hospitalized, I haven't been able to lie on my stomach. This is nice. I can nestle here until Pete arrives, which should be soon, or I could jump up and put together breakfast. Jump up, what a nice thought. I wait for his knock, nothing. Five minutes more, nothing.

What if I grab a shower, dress, and then make breakfast? In less than twenty minutes I peer into the refrigerator and cupboards for what's available. Unbelievable; an unopened box of Frosted Mini-Wheats. I put breakfast together; bowls out, spoons are out, milk out, napkins out. Orange juice poured. Coffee brewing. A soft knock on the door.

"Come in."

"Good morning, Mike. How are you?"

"I'm great. Hey Pete, do you make the bed?"

"Nope."

"It makes itself?"

"In a manner of speaking."

"Did you cook breakfast yesterday?"

"More like I assembled it. The stove is for show. Remember, with decoding no need to process anything to get from beginning to end, from farm to table as it were."

"I'm beginning to understand that." I nod toward the dining table. "Breakfast? I assembled it myself. By the way, is eating necessary here?"

"Breakfast, yes, thank you and no, we don't have to eat. But we can and it's enjoyable to do so. No need to drink either, but that's enjoyable too."

"Noted. All part of the adjustment."

We sit at the table as always except for last night's pizza. I continue, "What's on tap today?"

"You wander around connecting with people. It can be anyone, from anywhere and from any time-period. You've taken a look at the physical universe, now you can explore the people side. The task for the moment is to get a better perspective on life and thus nonlife."

"I like that."

Pete reaches into his shirt pocket and pulls out a pen and small notepad and hands them to me. "Take your coffee and this to the sofa, give it some thought and write out a list of who you'd like to see."

I list twenty names, cross out ten and add another twenty. After crossing out and adding a number of times I finalize a list of ten and hand it to Pete.

"You know," he says. "You can list a hundred if you like."

"I thought that, but ten is a good start."

"Top of the list, your parents."

"Yeah, I want to see what they were like as children.

Give me a sense of where I came from."

"Nice." Pete scrunches his eyes. "'The guy who invented the wheel?'"

"Can I do that?"

"Sure. Why?"

"Hugely curious about the guy who made such an important discovery. Want to find out how he did it."

"Great. Now Shakespeare. That one I get."

"Greatest understanding of people and the best writer in English history."

"Abraham Lincoln. Right. Freud?"

"I was a psychology minor. Have to talk to Freud about life and death."

"Rosa Parks."

"A most courageous woman. Did so much for civil rights."

"Ben Franklin, greatest American inventor, statesman, you name it and he did it. Nice. Helen Keller."

"I want to understand how she learned to communicate as she did. Impossible achievements."

"Picasso."

I begin clearing the breakfast dishes from the table as I respond. "How did he go from realistic portraits to cubism? He was such a talented portrait artist."

"Nice list. I'm aware of one or two more that may appeal to you."

"Who?"

"How about Jesus or Mohammed?"

"Neither occurred to me."

"Many people would like to talk to one of them, or both, or others. Abraham comes to mind; as do Adam and

Eve and perhaps other people from the Bible."

"I'll think about it. Is my list doable?"

"Absolutely. Do you want to go to them or have them come to you?"

"I will go to them. How does this work?"

"They will take the lead and define who you are. There will be no problems of identity, age, language, clothing, nothing. You will seamlessly fit into their every-day lives. I want to be clear on this. You will fit into their lives. They are not holograms or images or shadows or robots or dead and in Heaven. You are joining their lives as they lived them. All you do is show up."

I sit back at the table.

"That makes it easy."

"What did you expect?"

"I'm in Heaven and I'm learning."

"Yes, you are. Ready to start?"

"I am."

"Like to visit your mom first?"

We're sitting on a log in the playground of an elementary school my mother and me. I'm a schoolboy in short pants, holding a mimeographed questionnaire in one hand and a chewed-up pencil in the other. Dozens of other kids dash around, yelling, climbing on the jungle gym, playing baseball and otherwise in full recess mode. My mother is wearing a light colored long-sleeve blouse under a dark brown vest and a gray, knee length skirt, gray socks and badly scuffed shoes.

"Now you ask me the questions," she says.

The paper form has ten questions with spaces for the answers. I can smell the sweetness of the ink.

"Where and when were you born?"

"San Diego, California. October 7th, 1910."

"What is your favorite color?"

"Green."

"What is the most important thing to happen in your lifetime?"

"Women can vote."

"What is your greatest accomplishment?"

She pauses for a moment. I can't help but stare. My mother, twelve years old. Cute, smart, smelling of lavender. So serious, concentrating on the questions. My mother was my emotional rock, now she's delicate, exuberant, all girl. My heart melts. I'm almost in tears.

"I know. It was winning the tap dancing contest last year. I love to dance and that was my first contest. I was nervous but got over it."

"What is the most important thing in your life?" I didn't care about her answers, just hearing her voice meant everything.

"My family. I have an older brother, a younger brother and a younger sister. My mother bakes wonderful apple pies and my father works in a grocery store. My grandmother lives with us too."

I held up my hand for her to slow down. She is talking faster than I can write. Ready again. I want this to last forever.

"If you could change one thing in the world, what would it be?"

"They wouldn't fight in wars anymore. My uncle died

in one when I was seven."

A girl screams, a fingernail on the blackboard screech. My mother doesn't look up; just a normal playground sound to her. I look up. I had forgotten how screechy little girls can be. Back to my mother's fragrance, her curly hair and her earnestness. I am sitting with my mother as she is on the cusp of becoming a young woman. This little girl gave me life.

"What do you want to do when you grow up?"

"I want to be a nurse. I want to help sick people."

"Do you want a family?"

"Oh yes. I want a husband who is president of a bank and we will have four children, just like my family. And grandparents will live with us too. I want a two-story house with a basement and an automobile and a telephone."

She sits patiently while I finish writing.

"What makes people happy?"

"People are happy when other people are nice to them. People are sad when other people are mean to them."

"What does God do?"

"He protects us and loves us and helps us love each other."

The bell rings to end recess, my mother jumps up and runs back to class with the other children. I watch her disappear through the school doors and for the briefest moment I am melancholy. Here she is thoughtful, eager, but so unassuming; a little girl that would grow up to protect me from harm, encourage me when I was down, believe in me when I didn't believe in myself. I was so lucky.

Then I am back at my new home where Pete sits on the couch waiting to hear what happened.

"It was wonderful," I tell him. "I got to see her, hear her voice, smell the kid she was; lavender and dirt."

"Did you learn something?"

"Not sure I wanted to learn from her. I wanted a better sense of who she was. I loved connecting with her as a child. But something happened near the end of the visit. I felt sad, sad about people growing up, being disappointed, losing their innocence. I didn't think bad feelings are allowed in Heaven."

"All feelings can be experienced here, but negative ones are rare, mild and short-lived, and I think that one might be more positive than negative. A lot of love there."

"When my mother was alive, we didn't talk about her childhood much. I wish we had. Same with my dad."

"Want to connect with him now?

"Yes."

I'm sitting behind a big wooden desk in what looks like an office. A bookcase stands against the wall to my left and wooden chairs line the right-hand wall. Opposite my desk is a wooden door with a frosted glass window. It's a school office. There isn't a mirror, but I'm wearing a suit and can tell by looking at my hands I am an older adult. I wonder if I'm the principal. I'm excited to see my dad. Three raps on the door's window announce his arrival.

"Come in."

A scruffy boy about twelve enters, grabs a chair from the right wall, places it in front of the desk as if he had done so a hundred times and drops into the chair. His shirt, tight across the chest and inches above his wrists, is held together with patches.

"I suppose you realize why you are here," I say, acting as a principal when I'm captivated looking at the boy that will become my dad.

"Yes sir. Fighting."

"Explain what happened, please." I can be the principal and enamored at the same time. Like with my mother, I'm almost in tears again.

"It wasn't my fault. Donald called my dad a dirty miner."

"Your dad is a miner and miners get dirty."

My dad is silent.

"How many times have you been to this office for fighting?"

"Don't know."

"Too many. This has to stop. You're headed toward expulsion." I say that, but want to hug the little guy before this ends.

"I'm quitting next year anyway. It won't make no difference."

"You plan to work in the mines?"

"What else am I going to do?"

"Do you think you're being smart?"

"I'm not sassing anyone."

"No. I mean intelligent. Are you making an intelligent decision?"

"I don't know."

"Do you like living in Thurmond?"

He gives me a glance as if I were the dumbest person walking on the face of the earth. What a kid.

"No."

"How about West Virginia?"

"No."

"Where would you like to live?"

"California."

"What's in California?"

"Movie stars. The ocean. Palm trees."

"Sounds nice. How are you going to get there?"

"I ain't. I'm going to work in the mines."

I feel sorry for the boy. He turns out well, but I hate to see his despair. There is nothing I can do, or is there? I am not too sure about this time travel bit.

"You don't want to work in the mines?"

"Don't matter what I want."

My dad did make it to California where he met my mom and got busy creating me after a couple of practice kids.

"What did your father want? Did he want to work in the mines?"

"Don't know."

"What can I tell you so you'll stop fighting?"

"Don't know."

"Do you like fighting?"

"No."

"You fight with Donald and the others because they make fun of your father being a miner?"

"I guess."

"When they tease you and you fight and get in trouble, they win."

"I clock 'em pretty good."

I have to muffle my laugh. I like my dad as a kid, full of spirit, not going to back down to anybody. There is nothing I have to do. He would toughen up, but remain the gentle man who was my father. I'm not aware of him meeting a movie star, but we swam in the ocean and had palm trees in our front yard in San Diego. I wondered what attracted my mom to him. They met in their early twenties, he four years older. He escaped Thurmond, West Virginia by joining the navy. And captured my mother's heart while stationed in San Diego. He was discharged prior to World War II, but re-upped after Pearl Harbor. After the war, he attended college on the G.I. Bill earning an engineering degree and a job at Convair, a long way from the coalmines.

"Will you do me a favor?"

"What?"

"Next time, before you throw a punch, would you imagine a palm tree next to the ocean for only two seconds?" I want to help, but realize he doesn't need it.

He sits straighter in his chair. "I can do that."

"Good. Now return to your class. And put away your chair."

Smiling with pride for my dad, I watch him open the door. As soon as the door closes, I am home again.

"What a kid. He was all boy and on the way to becoming quite a man. I wasn't aware of the deep roots that held him in place. His father worked the mines, and his grand-father and probably his great grandfather. That was only an historical fact to me, not the uncompromising future it was to him. By the way, what was I seeing, talking to, an image of some sort?"

"Your dad. I tried to tell you earlier. You're not doing time travel. You were talking to your dad. Not an image. Not a projection or hologram or anything else. That was your dad living his life and you were talking to him, same as with your mom."

"You're right, I don't get it. Didn't I go back in time to when he was a kid?"

"No, you traveled to where he is a kid."

"I traveled to where he is a kid."

"You say that with such conviction, such confidence."

"I went to a where not a when. To where he is, not was, a kid."

"Yes."

"So, he was real."

"Yes."

"Everything's real."

"Now you're getting it."

"When you say not 'when' but 'where' is that some-thing like space-time, folding space, that kind of thing?"

"Yes, that kind of thing."

"Okay. It's coming together. I want to visit the guy inventing the wheel."

I climb a small rise, moving away from a river and toward distant hills. On my left are trees, a mix of beech, fir and oak. To the right, perhaps a quarter mile away, is a village of a hundred wooden huts. From the top of the rise I view a narrow swale where a woman chops on the end of a small log. The ax head appears to be either copper or bronze. Two wooden wheels lean against a rock.

I expected a man, a caveman. This woman is clean, comfortably dressed in a cloth robe and smiles when she sees me. I expected grunts, she asks me a question.

"You, boy, are you here to help?"

I raise my hand; startled to see the hand of a young boy.

"Yes, sister, if I can. I am curious to understand how this works."

I'm probably eight years old. I called her "sister" although I don't think she is my sister. My guess is that it's a term for unmarried females of the village; I don't know why I think that. I run down the slope to where she stands.

She hands me an ax. "We need to narrow this part to fit into the hole." She gestures first to the log and next to the hole in each wheel. "The problem," she continues, "is that the log has to be big enough to be strong, but thin enough to fit into the hole and not get too hot from rubbing or too loose either. We're close."

I chop at my end, but it is slow going. The wood is hard and my ax is soft and dull. After a while, she motions to stop and rest on nearby rocks. It's lunchtime. We share bread she pulls from a bag and water from a clay jug.

"How long have you been working on this?" I ask.

"Long time. We need a way to carry heavy loads up and down the hills. I had a toy with these, but the center part turned. I wanted to build a large one with the center part being still to hold a load. This might be the day it works."

"It looks like it will work soon. I'm afraid my end is not ready."

"I will finish your end and we can put it together when I am done."

She chops and hacks on my end for another half hour while I watch her and gaze at my surroundings. We're in a river valley nestled maybe five miles from a series of rolling hills. I have no idea where we are in the world, but I can see cultivated fields and they have a degree of civilization based on the size of the village. And they communicate through a developed language. This is not caveman days.

"Ready."

She holds the chopped log, waiting next to one of the wheels. I hold the wheel upright while she fits the log into the hole. Once in, she shoves a wooden peg into a hole near the end of the log to hold it in place and ties it down. We do the same with the other wheel and stand back to see two wheels and an axle, although I don't know what she would label them. I'm watching one of the great moments in history.

"Sit on the log and I will push you to determine if it works."

I sit on the log axle and she pushes. The log, a bit wobbly, catches on the turning wheels, but stays steady enough for me to remain balanced: A fantastic invention, but impractical as it is. While I watch from the side, she attaches two thick poles to the log near the wheels and binds them together in the front, making a triangle. She ties smaller sticks across the triangle to create a load-bearing platform. She designed and built the first cart and is moving it back and forth, testing it.

"It works." She glances over to me. "I will take this to the village and try it with bags of grain."

I wave goodbye as she pulls her invention up the small hill toward her village. Once she arrives, the world will change. While sitting on a rock as I love to do, I reflect on what I have seen.

First, this place is beautiful. The sun had crossed the sky while we worked and is now descending toward the hills. Shadows grow and the air is cooling quickly.

Second, the wheel was invented far later in history than I realized and by a woman.

Third, perhaps the greatest invention of all time is a simple handcart made of wood and brought into the bosom of civilization by pulling it into a commonplace village alongside a river. I imagine within weeks nearby villages will roll their own fleets of carts over the hills.

Fourth, from the desire to carry more weight from place to place, the lives of billions of people will improve.

And last, I am indeed fortunate to find myself in Heaven. I am ready to go back.

Pete sits on the couch, two glasses of wine on the coffee table.

"Well?"

"Did you realize the wheel was invented by a woman?"

"I did not."

"Do you know where it was invented?"

"Don't know that either, but I suppose we could find out."

"Doesn't matter. What's important is how simple contributing to the betterment of humankind can be. Doesn't have to be complex or monumental or fix a big problem. The wheel was created to carry heavy loads up a hill. That's it. And in a regular old place, not a big city or hub of knowledge; and I'm guessing central Europe. It seemed like a nice place with nice people. Oh, she mentioned that the men of the village were proud of the weight they could carry up a hill. I can picture men struggling under huge sacks and her sauntering by with her cart loaded with double what they could carry. Inflated male egos punctured by female smarts."

"You're glad you went."

"It was fantastic."

"Had enough for today? It's late."

"How long was I gone?"

Pete laughs. "Mike, I've been trying to teach you about time. Time means nothing here. For now, time is what we want it to be."

"How much time did I take anyway? I like time."

"An hour and two minutes."

"How...?"

"Just long enough for me to watch Laurel and Hardy in 'A Chump at Oxford.' One of my favorites. I love early mass media comedy. Give me Laurel and Hardy, Chaplin, Abbott and Costello and most of the early TV comics and I'm as jolly as a squirting lapel flower."

"I had no idea. It is early for you, but you want it to be late for me."

"Yes and the reason is to keep you sane. Too many changes too quickly would not be good. If you had been an experienced space-time traveler, there would be no problem. But you're not. You're a normal human being."

"What a strange thing, to be encoded and decoded."

"No stranger than how one needle on a record player can reproduce every instrument of a symphony orchestra."

"I've never understood that either."

Pete gets up. "I've left you dinner in the oven. I will return in the morning. Tomorrow is an important day, a day, one might say, of great purpose."

Day
4

Purpose

Sleep didn't come easily last night. Now I'm healthy and can move again, I tossed and turned wondering why I ended up in Heaven to face eternity, an eternity that before had been dark and silent. A week or two of orientation will determine my forever. Shouldn't that be God's job? Judging a lifetime of my actions? Those with faith have little to fear; live a good life and God will say "welcome." Those of us who stick with science sure are stuck when we arrive in the hereafter. My life was supposed to have a beginning, a middle and an end. I was a product of my time, but not for all time, and I must admit that whatever I chose to do in life was not so profound that I couldn't leave it for someone else to finish. Everyone making it to Heaven means earthly life has no purpose. Just put in the time until you die and the fun starts. Why bother with the life part? Where does purpose come from?

Then I feel it again, that nagging anxiety rising and growing fangs. Something isn't right and I'm not sure I should disclose that to Pete.

After breakfast, I tell Pete only that I want to talk with Helen Keller. No one had overcome more adversity. If I meet with her when she is older, after she learned how to read lips by touching them, I'm sure we can communicate well enough and I can learn about purpose. Pete, being Pete, says, "I will make it so," and flashes the Vulcan hand salute.

I am led into a home office or library by a studious young woman who instructs me to sit on the center cushion of a couch. The décor is old-fashioned, knickknacks on many surfaces, lace curtains on the windows. One wall is a built-in bookcase filled with large-sized books, likely printed in braille. The couch itself has exposed carved wooden arms partially covered with padding and fabric. It's a comfortable, elderly aunt's room.

I sit only a moment before Miss Keller enters. She looks wonderful, closer to pretty than handsome. Short white hair is tight to her head. Without hesitation she walks to me, holds out her hand and says, "Good morning."

I stand to shake her hand and without further ado, she sits next to me.

First order of business is to make sure I can communicate with her. She, however, takes charge.

"I understand you write for your college newspaper. I'm happy to answer your questions. We can talk if you speak your words clearly. I will touch your lips and listen with my fingers."

Her speech is a bit difficult to follow, but we should

be fine. She touches my lips.

"I want to understand how you learned after losing your sight and hearing before you were even two years old."

She puts her hand in her lap. I wondered what she would do to tell me it was her turn to speak.

"I was angry when I learned people could talk with their mouths. I was about five years old and had no idea what talking was, but soon learned it was a way to share thoughts and I couldn't do that well. I had to pantomime what I wanted to say. It was hard. I hated being unable to talk and I must confess I wasn't pleasant to be around in those days."

She touches my lips; she is finished and I am to respond. I want to keep my questions short.

"Did you feel trapped?"

"More than trapped. Cheated. There was a world I could not join. It got worse and worse. I was fuming. And then Anne Sullivan entered my life. Her real name was Joanne, my family found her, hoping she would help me. She was blind too, for a while. First, she was my governess, then my teacher and my friend. We attended college together, The Perkins Institute, Wright-Humason School and Radcliffe. She was the one who taught me about letters making words. From that point on, you couldn't stop me. Unfortunately, she became blind again and died too young."

"Was she your inspiration?"

"Oh no. She was my door to a new world, but I pushed my way through it, doing all the work to learn how to read, to hear others, to speak myself because I was driven.

I wanted to participate, not sit by and let the world exist without me."

"You accomplished a lot."

"You are kind. One of my important efforts was for women's suffrage. It made me mad that women could not vote. How does that make sense? A good angry can go a long way if it is channeled and not allowed to burst all over the place. I was also pleased how many new organizations helped the blind. It seems our efforts for the blind spilled over for other groups too. Our country should do what is needed for every citizen, especially the ones who cannot compete equally with others. In truth, I was lucky. I had intelligence, strong will, an able teacher and a need to achieve. Most people aren't blessed with all that. Not their fault."

"Did you accomplish what you set out to do?"

"More to do yet, the good Lord willing. I'm only eighty-one. I can read and I can write. I am aware of what is happening in the world and can share my thoughts and perhaps change a few minds. I'm concerned about civil rights. I worry about war."

She pauses as the young woman who seated me arrives carrying a tea service. The woman poured one cup and added lemon before asking me how I liked mine. She makes my cup and walks toward the door.

Helen turns to face the woman, "Thank you, Lisa." And turns back to me. "If you're wondering, I asked for tea and knew it arrived when I could smell Lisa's rose petal perfume."

"Can other people do what you do and have done?"

"Of course, but as I said, I was driven by frustration,

by anger and luckily Anne entered my life. She helped me survive. I'm not sure if my abilities were the best ones to succeed. They were the ones I had and the ones I had to use. I believe everyone has abilities, some not many, others perhaps enjoy an excess. It is too bad we're not all equally blessed, but that is what life is. It isn't fair, but much can be achieved when we do it together. Success comes from ability and from effort, and often with the encouragement and support of others."

"Miss Keller, I need to go soon. Any final thoughts for me?"

"Only that I hope this old lady had a useful word or two. Perhaps I provided you with a few ideas that will help you live your life to the fullest. How you define that is up to you. But recognize you can always do more. You must fight sometimes, but fight so you can give. Contribute to others in your life and you will be doing the best you can."

"Thank you, Miss Keller. It has been a pleasure."

I find myself back with Pete. I need a moment to settle down and Pete seems to sense that and remains quiet. Helen's fingers on my lips were both firm and tender. At no other time was I better listened to and she couldn't hear a word. I like her anger with direction. Can get a lot done if you're driven and focused at the same time.

"Well, Pete, that was fantastic. I admired her before, but after speaking with her, she has to be one of the world's greatest people."

"She did great things in spite of great challenges."

"In spades. I can't believe I talked with Helen Keller. She understood every word I said. I wonder what she could have done if she wasn't blind and deaf."

"Really?"

"What are you implying?"

"It doesn't work that way. Life is you, however you are, the decisions you make and what you do. If you were different, everything else would be different. Helen did what she did precisely because she was blind and deaf. Without those limitations, she might have ended up an English teacher, and a strict one at that. As Heraclitus said, 'No man ever steps into the same river twice, for it's not the same river and he's not the same man.' It's not the exact equivalent, but you get the idea."

"You are really an encyclopedia. Got the idea; life is what you decide and do, because of and in spite of hurdles. And, if I'm interpreting you right, life is effort and life is change and contentment comes after achievement. Heaven seems to be contentment all the time, no effort necessary. Doesn't feel quite right. Anyway, I'm ready to talk with someone else. Herr Doktor Sigmund Freud, bitte."

Another surprise. I expected to meet Dr. Freud in his Victorian consulting room, stuffed with art objects, oriental rugs and his famous couch. Instead, we're walking on a dirt path in a wooded park, most likely in London, since the few signs I can see are in English. This must be after he left Nazi Austria for England. We're in the last year of his life when he was in significant pain from cancer of the jaw. We stroll along the path, his steps short, aided by a cane. My interest is not in his development of psychoanalysis, but his upcoming suicide by morphine administered by his physician. I had contemplated something similar myself, before I ended up dead. His thoughts about making such a purposeful decision that ends all possibilities would help me better understand life and death and what lies ahead for me.

"Doctor Freud, thank you for meeting with me."

"The pleasure is mine." He lowers his head and touches the bill of his hat. "How may I be of service?"

"You're aware I talked with Dr. Schur about your plan when and if the pain becomes intolerable. I had been toying with the same idea myself..."

"Toying? Death is a serious consideration. One does not toy with it."

"I'm sorry. That was a bad choice of words. I wanted to better understand your thoughts on euthanasia."

"That is a broad subject. In what particulars are you interested?"

"The right to die. Specifically, does a person have the right to choose death; what circumstances and what state of mind enables a person to make such a significant and absolute decision?"

"As your Benjamin Franklin once said, 'nothing is sure except death and taxes.' Since the government forces us to pay taxes, we the people should be able to control the other surety, our deaths. Now I make a joke." He chuckles, then becomes serious. "However, to consider your concern."

With that, Dr. Freud makes the case for his point of view. He starts with the government's position that suicide is not a fundamental right and it is in a country's interest that people stay alive. Governments are obligated to monitor health care and protect against abusive, incompetent, and unscrupulous medical practices. Assisted suicide is the top of a slippery slope to profound abuses. Physicians, he adds, accept the sacred obligation to support life and must always support life and what that entails. Then he considers religion. No religion can support euthanasia, he says, only God can control man's time on earth.

On the other hand, he continues, who should command a person's life? Should any government, any church, any other person presume dominion over me? The government demands what is good for all the people. A religion mandates what is acceptable to their particular God. And other authorities expect compliance because of their own fears and agendas.

By this time, we reach a concrete pond where boys sail their toy boats. We rest on a bench among the trees; the wind rustling the leaves above us and watch the boys for a time and the other passersby, men wearing fedoras and women the long dresses common in the late 1930s. Doctor Freud looks wistful, as if trying to absorb the moment.

"I have not answered your question yet, but I will now. Most people possess sufficient self-awareness to consider this life-ending alternative. The effort of governing bodies, secular and religious, to control the individual in this matter is misplaced. For a competent person, who is in pain, who can foresee no improvement, but only more pain, the option to end one's life is a reasonable one. To me, the right to die, if not a legal right, remains a personal and moral right. For whom does this right apply? My answer is anyone in unrelenting pain who has decided enough is enough."

He pauses and we both observe the boys play with their boats. Most of them scurry along the shore, staying as close to their boats as possible, sometimes maneuvering them with sticks. Some just stand and watch. Freud continues.

"Those boys. Many push with sticks, others view from one place at the water's edge. Participate, observe, it is the same. But life grows narrow, more difficult to find a place, to take part. Those in emotional pain, severe enough and unrelenting enough, retain the right to this option. Medicines can help individuals cope with physical pain and to a degree emotional pain, but are limited in their positive effects and overbearing in their side effects, enough to provide unfortunates only brief and insufficient respite."

"How did you come to your personal decision?"

"First, I determined my health will not improve. There is no more my physicians can do except prescribe higher doses of pain medication which cloud my senses. Second, I determined my quality of life can only decline. Third, I reflected on my life and was satisfied. I had done what was reasonable for me to do. Fourth, I discussed with my family, my colleagues, and my friends these findings and received their support. Fifth, when I decided to end my life I enjoyed the luxury of contentment. And last, I have lived with this decision for a few months and it sits well.

"You see those boys playing with their boats? I do not own a boat anymore and I can no longer play. It is that simple. I learned that when a dog can no longer be a dog, it's time to let him go. Life should be worth living. When it is not, the individual should have choices no matter how much time might be left; quality, not quantity and no one else is qualified to judge quality but the individual."

"Doctor Freud, the individual should control his own life and death?"

"Without question."

"What about those who may not be rational?"

"Who is to say? Let us walk back along the path as we examine these important questions. Is the government, any government, knowledgeable enough to decide what an individual experiences and what he should do with those experiences? The answer is no. Should any church that worships a god other respected churches do not believe in claim dominion over any and every individual? No. Does any doctor, any lawyer or citizens of any rank grasp what is best for any and every individual? No. Can a psychotic understand enough of his life to rightfully end it? The answer is yes. Can the everyday man? The answer is again yes.

"The decision is not that monumental. I will give away a few months of my existence and gain peace. A psychotic may give away years, but these will be years of torment, misunderstanding and unhappiness. Who is to say what is good and not good? Only the individual."

At this point we rest on another park bench.

"Doctor Freud, thank you for today and thank you for your books. I studied your work, as have many others. You opened many doors and helped countless people."

"Thank you. You are kind to say so."

"Any questions for me?"

He smiles. "Are you going make the decision?"

I look into the face of Sigmund Freud and tell him the truth.

"My circumstances changed. I am no longer ill, no longer in pain."

"That is good to hear," he nods his head. "I'm glad. Let us continue on our way."

Somewhere between the bench and the exit from the park, I lose Doctor Freud.

I'm back on the couch.

"Well," Pete asks, "Are you still blaming your mother?"

Pete is setting me up with one of the classic psychoanalytic questions. I respond with what I remember of Freud's rival Alfred Adler's theory of birth order. "I've never blamed my mother. She was great, as was my dad. I blame my siblings for most of my problems. Without them I would have been the favored only child." Pete didn't respond to what I thought was a witty and learned reply. Maybe it wasn't as witty or learned as I thought. Ah well.

"Did you get what you wanted from the good doctor?"

"Yes. I wanted to understand how he could justify ending his life. He seemed to say life can expire before actual physical death and to consider ending it early is reasonable. He didn't say that exactly, but that's what I took away. And, I liked the guy. He wasn't aloof, professorial. More like a favorite uncle, brilliant of course, but warm and engaging too."

"You still interested in seeing more people?"

"Oh yeah."

"Who's next?"

"Ben Franklin. He will help me better understand human potential and thus how well I did with my life."

I'm standing at the rail of a frigate. It sports three masts, at least forty cannons and is pitching in heavy seas; blue-green rollers windblown into whitecaps as far as the horizon which is thick with storm clouds. We're traveling from France back to the U.S. or what will become the U.S. I don't know how I know that, I just do. I know things I have no reason to. Which makes me wonder why I don't know more. I'm dead and in Heaven, why don't I know everything?

Ben Franklin: raconteur, Minister to France, creator of libraries, Poor Richard's Almanac, Postmaster General, explorer of electricity, inventor of the lightning rod and bifocals, abolitionist, honorary degrees from Harvard and Yale, co-drafter of the Declaration of Independence and a signer of the American Constitution. I probably know as much about him as anyone after reading his short autobiography and a half dozen thick biographies. But I hesitate. As I stand at the rail, my heart is thumping. Breathing is quick. I'm light headed. I'm afraid again. This can't be right. I have to stop.

I'm back at the abode reaching for the glass of iced tea Pete is handing to me.

"Pizza is warming in the oven. What's up? That was a short visit. I had only enough time to listen to 'Who's on First.'"

"'What's up?' No. What's on second."

Pete laughs. "You know the skit!"

"I love Abbott and Costello. Yes, I'm back. Something wasn't right. Given the circumstances, this is going to sound weird. While waiting to see Mr. Franklin, I realized my efforts to make sense of being dead and being in Heaven were intellectual. I'm trying to grasp life and death with my head and not my feelings. Life is doing and feeling, not just thinking. Ben Franklin would have been more ideas and I need more life. I'm stuck in neutral and need to feel what life is again; that's the weird part. I can see Ben later. Can I do something now that will help me sense life rather than think life?"

"Of course. This is Heaven, everything's possible. I've got an idea. Trust me?"

"With my life."

"Funny."

"What's your idea?"

"You liked to hike; one of your favorite pastimes, right?"

"Yup."

"Did you do any mountaineering?"

"Small time stuff, some belaying and rappelling, brief exposure on climbs, but nothing outrageous."

"Well, I present the climb of climbs to you. You'll be as alive as you've ever experienced. There is gear in the closet. Get yourself put together and I'll send you off."

The closet holds mountain climbing equipment, including, ominously, crampons and oxygen bottles. I get into the gear, pizza forgotten and stand by the door.

"I set you up to climb Mount Everest, beginning seven hundred feet below the summit. Open the door and have fun."

I hunch under gale force winds at the bottom of a forty-foot tower of ice and rock, snow hitting me like small stones. It's Hillary's Step, a bottleneck that can delay climbers for hours with those going up bumping into those going down on an exposed spur that scarcely holds one person. I'm alone, with ropes already in place. My job is to hoist myself up and over. As I look up, I'm reminded of the rope climb in high school with the addition of wind, ice and rock, bulky clothes, oxygen bottles, crampons, and heavy mitts. I half climb on the ice and rocks and half pull myself up the rope. Somehow my strength expands to meet the demands of Hillary's Step and I lie on my stomach catching my breath at the top. I'm already suffering the effects of the thin atmosphere. I can hardly breathe.

The rest of the climb will be more of a challenge: the exposure of falling thousands of feet if I slip; the wind blowing hard enough to knock me down, the below zero cold and the lack of oxygen which my oxygen bottle barely dents.

I climb a snowy ridge moving one foot just in front of the other, advancing not much more than the length of my boot. The dry snow crackles with each step. I take three breaths: inhale-exhale, inhale-exhale, inhale-exhale, then take another step. With head lowered against the wind and cold, I force this labored assent for two minutes at a time, then rest two minutes. It is necessary to go slow, and critical not to delay. Hundreds have lost their lives at this death zone elevation, most from simple mistakes in an unforgiving environment. Often bodies are left where the climber collapsed, recovering them being far too dangerous for those who would help. Some are abandoned while still alive.

What's to enjoy from head down climbing a mountain in a blizzard? Breathing is labored. The body is exhausted and if you make it to the top, which most do not, you still must descend. I slow to one step and four breaths. I rest after one minute instead of two. Yet I push on. Ahead is a ridge. I climb that and look upward. From that ridge top I see another, fifty yards distant. That's my next target. The ridge after that is closer, thirty yards. I climb that. Now I rest after every three steps. The next ridgeline is only twenty yards away. It takes fifteen minutes to reach it, but when I do, I look over the opposite side of Everest. I am on the summit.

The wind buffets me side to side. I crouch; uncertain I can rise again, and look over the horizon from the top of the world. My platform is not much, ten feet in diameter but safe. Below me a hundred mountain peaks poke out of the clouds into the thin blue of the sky. I kneel in the snow and turn for a panoramic view. Never have I felt so alive. Like those before me, I don't linger at the top.

Descending is not as easy as I expected. Fatigue has saturated my muscles and bones. My oxygen-assisted brain can't concentrate. It would be easy to walk off an edge or slip, hurt myself and be unable to continue. Being unable to continue means freezing and dying. I wonder what would become of me if I make a mistake. Can I die twice?

Carefully, I descend Hillary's Step. It is as difficult going down as it was climbing. I keep slipping off the face and have to grab at the ropes. Finally, my boots crunch on the bottom. At that point, I am whisked back.

Still shivering with cold, I remove my gear while Pete waits on a chair.

"None the worse for wear, I take it?" This time Pete offers a cup of hot tea.

"That was perfect." I relax on the couch, now warm and in shorts and a T-shirt, sipping my tea. Chocolate chip cookies are arranged on a plate on the coffee table. "I've no idea how people can do that for real."

"What do you mean? You did it for real."

"Yeah, the last few hundred feet without the earlier climbing and days of depletion from breathing the thin air."

"Do you want to go back and do it from the beginning? We can do that."

"No, no. I'm good."

"Find what you were looking for?"

"Yes. I wanted to feel life again. I did that. In fact, I was in fear for my life up there. Which is weird since I'm dead. Not sure what the difference is between being alive on earth and being dead in Heaven. I don't understand what dead is anymore."

"You said earlier, contentment, curiosity and confusion."

"I guess I've lost sight of the purpose."

"Of Heaven?"

"Yeah. It's like fun and games. I can do whatever I want. What am I doing here?"

"You are exploring Heaven, getting your bearings, creating information so you can forever delight in the hereafter."

"Creating information. Does that mean providing information to all those dimensions?"

"Yes. It takes a while to fit you to Heaven and fit Heaven to you."

"We need to talk more about that. The other concern of the afterlife is the absence of reward and punishment. If there is no reward or punishment, what's the purpose of life and the afterlife?"

"Why does either need a purpose? When you were alive, and an atheist, I imagine you believed life didn't have any greater purpose. Life just was. Correct?"

"Not exactly. Life in general didn't have a purpose, but my individual life had to have one. I made sure of that. I had to find a reason to get out of bed in the morning."

"Is that why you are searching for a purpose now?"

"I think so, and here's why. If an afterlife exists, there must be a purpose to it and only if the afterlife has a purpose, can life have a purpose."

"Why can't Heaven be an extension of a person's life? No questions asked."

"I'm listening."

"And for a person's first experiences in Heaven, he or she explores life and death as necessary so that Heaven can enhance that person's Heavenly experience."

I reach for a second chocolate chip cookie. The combination of exhaustion, relief from the fear of falling to my death off Mount Everest, steaming tea with a dollop of two-percent milk and a pile of warm chocolate chip cookies is truly Heaven. I sink deeper in the chair as my body relaxes into stage-four contentment. By what remains on the plate, Pete must be on his third or fourth cookie.

"And every person goes to Heaven?"

"Yes."

"Even babies?"

"Ah, no. Not all babies. Once a child has developed a sufficient sense of self-awareness, for our purposes around five or six months of age, they are able to enter Heaven after they die. Has to do with relevant information points. Until cell migration to the frontal lobes is complete in an infant, a whole, individualized human being doesn't exist. We use science to define the individual, not conception, not a heartbeat, or twenty weeks gestation, or pain sensation or anything else. Biological existence isn't our starting point, a self and self-awareness is."

"That's a discomforting approach. Innocent babies have nowhere to go? What happens to aliens, people from other planets?"

"If they are intelligent and self-aware and they die, they're here."

"Can I meet one?"

"Sure. Not now, but later."

"How much longer until I create enough data to forever delight in the hereafter?"

"You're coming along fine. Another few days. Remember, the norm is a week or two."

"How long does a Pope take?"

"The last one took six hours."

"Six hours?"

"Yeah. He spent his whole life figuring things out and was prepared for everything he faced. Just a few double-checks and off he goes."

"Adolph Hitler? How long did he take?"

"Want to guess?"

"Six months."

"Six hours."

"You're kidding."

"Nope. Hitler was the same as the Pope. Knew everything, although he was wrong, but the strength of his convictions in life created enough data that he didn't need more. A few double-checks for him and off he goes too."

"Hard to believe."

"Your life didn't prepare you well to land here. But you're doing great exploring the issues."

"Pete, here's where I am at the moment. I want to comprehend how a life is measured. I appreciate it's not length. How long a person lives means little. What does mean something? There are three possibilities as I figure it. One is that there is no meaning; no purpose which leads to concluding there is nothing to measure. Two is what a person does in one lifetime is the measure and then it's done. Nowhere to go but the grave. Three is the measure of living the kind of life that gets you into Heaven. But since everyone gets into Heaven, that measure doesn't count. I'm left with me being the only one who can measure the value of my own existence from birth to death. I did that during my life so I don't need the gift of life extension provided by Heaven. I created meaning during my life and now I'm done."

"You're the only judge of the value of your life?"

"Absolutely. It's my life, my purpose, my measurement of right and wrong, good and bad. No doubt about that. In fact, that's the only thing that makes sense of my experience now. My data creates my Heaven, nobody else's."

Pete reaches for another cookie and says, "Another question. What do you measure?"

"I've given that considerable thought over the years. I always wondered about the validity of my values. I wasn't an Einstein or Freud, but I was good at being me; small stuff, being nice to people, doing the right thing. That's my measure; contributing as well as I could to others."

"Are you confident of the value of what you did?"

"I'm at ease, in part because I believe in a quote by Bertrand Russell, 'The whole problem with the world is that fools and fanatics are always so certain of themselves, and wiser people so full of doubts.' I'm comfortable with my doubts and trust I'm wise enough to assess my life. Even so, I'd like to start a second list of experiences, more involved than what I had today. I want to explore personal perspectives."

"Ready to list them now?"

"No. Let me mull over the possibilities and share with you tomorrow. Are you staying for dinner?"

"I could rustle up a mean spaghetti, garlic bread and

Chianti."

"Can you do music? I miss music."

"Sure. What's your pleasure?"

"Jazz."

"You got it."

Smooth jazz accompanies our dinner.

"When do I get to do the magical stuff? It seems about time I learn how to do the cool things."

"You can now. Imagine what you want in the right way and it will happen."

"What's the right way?"

"You'll figure it out."

After Pete leaves, I pour myself a nightcap and adjourn to the couch. With my feet on the coffee table, a smooth Scotch in my hand, and smooth jazz in the background I expect an evening of smooth mellowing beyond compare. It isn't happening. That deep-in-the-gut anxiety has risen higher and grown into fear, an ominous, unshakable fear that doesn't make sense.

Day
5

More Dying

Pete hasn't shown this morning. I have plenty of time to practice making things happen. First, I try to conjure a ham sandwich. Doesn't work. As Pete suggested, I think about it. What would make a ham sandwich appear? I have to want it. Could be I have to need it. I just had breakfast and I don't need a sandwich. I'd like another coffee. I think about a cup of coffee. None appears. There is coffee in the pot, five feet away. I don't need anything and I don't want anything. I'm in Heaven, what's to need and want?

I push myself up from the chair, pour myself another cup of coffee and return. This isn't magic, nothing tricky going on. Somehow, I must connect with the seven thousand dimensions. Yesterday someone or something provided Mount Everest and put me near the top. That was awesome, so was being on a ship with Ben Franklin waiting for me, and sitting and chatting with Helen Keller. I needed those things to help me make sense of dying and being in Heaven. A ham sandwich wouldn't help do that.

That could be the difference. Knowing what Beth is doing right now would help. I close my eyes and imagine my wife getting out of bed, moving around the kitchen making breakfast, sitting with family in the living room, and me wishing I could join her. Nothing. What do I need? What do I need? My task is to create data, indicators of who I am and what I'm about so I ascend to the totality of Heaven. Okay, a ham sandwich isn't data that would help me ascend anywhere and neither is my wife. I'm getting it. My wife is already a data point, or a whole slew of them as the center of my life.

Then fear ignites, rising, pushing contentment aside like lava driving toward the surface. Powerful. Irresistible. Horrifying. The same near panic about dying that clutched me so violently as a young man is again squeezing my chest. I'm afraid of dying. I fear dying more than I ever have. How can that be? Panic is swirling inside my head making me dizzy. I grab the arms of the chair and remind myself to breathe. I'm afraid of dying. I'm losing it. Take a sip of coffee. Calm down. Calm down. Must be old sensations coming back under these odd circumstances. All part of the first few days adjusting to being deceased. Within a minute I am normal again. I drink more coffee, take a deep breath and refocus on the task at hand, learning how to make things happen.

Alas, the first thing that comes to mind is being a spider. All my life, I didn't like spiders, I was afraid of them. No more than other people I suppose, but I had friends who picked them up in their bare hands without hesitation and carried them to safety outside. I pounded them five, six, seven times with the hardest objects nearby until they were flat and often in pieces. I regretted each time I did that. House spiders don't harm anyone. They are our friends; they eat bugs. I wished I was nicer to them. Worst for me was finding one in the shower. I'd stand as far away as possible, sometimes outside the shower and spray them until their legs folded up and they floated to the drain and around it a few times. I held the water on them until they slipped through a drain hole and down into the sewer system. I continued spraying for another few seconds to make sure they couldn't crawl back up while I was washing. I didn't want to do that, but I did it. On occasion in the bathroom I'd spot a tiny spider and let it live. But each time I entered the bathroom I'd look for the spider. If I found it in an out of the way place, okay. If I couldn't find it, I worried that it would appear, big, hairy and menacing when I was sitting on the toilet. After a few days I gave up being nice and declared war, allowing me to flatten that spider as soon as it appeared. I didn't like doing that either.

Sometimes I considered, in the interest of universal fairness, that if Heaven existed, I would be required to earn my entry through the Pearly Gates in part by enduring the harm I caused during life, most notably by me drowning as a spider in the shower as many times as the number I killed.

I sit in the chair, now relaxed, coffee finished, and consider becoming a spider in a shower stall.

I'm blind. Not blind exactly, I can see light, but nothing else. It is more like I can't focus. Next, I sense huge vibrations, the whole world is rocking. Pressure pushes down on my body and legs. I slide and keep sliding, my legs useless to stop me. Then sensations stop.

I am back in my room. As a spider murderer, I worried about the spider's fear and pain. Was I causing unfair distress to a harmless fellow creature? As I experienced it, the answer is no. That doesn't excuse doing it, but I can now consider my actions a little less malevolent.

I can't wait to tell Pete what I did. Oh gosh. I flash on another transgression, something I did in junior high school. It was an afternoon school dance in the cafeteria; the tables and chairs had been pushed back enabling the boys to huddle on one side and the girls to sit in a row on the other. We boys were out of our element and nervous. I told my friends to watch. I marched across the empty floor to one of the girls. "Do you want to dance?" I asked. As she began to rise I said, "You should ask Joe, maybe he wants to," and returned to my friends and we all laughed. What an obnoxious jerk I was.

How many times in my life had I been an obnoxious jerk? Less as I grew older, I hope. But how often have I hurt people unknowingly? No doubt a lot more often than I killed spiders. On the plus side, I remember many shopping trips with Beth where I would grab something too high or far back for her to reach. When that happened, I made it a point to bring forward the remaining items that other shoppers might not be able to reach. I'm really a nice guy. But I fear that my silent good deeds were far outnumbered by self-centeredness and ignorance.

A soft knock on the door announces Pete's arrival.

"Come in."

He relaxes on the couch while I explain my newfound knowledge and abilities and my recollections of obnoxiousness. All he asks is, "Can you create lunch? I'd like a salad, a chicken salad with honey mustard dressing."

I concentrate on how good it would be to create lunch, a chicken salad for Pete and a chop-chop salad for me, and to further take charge of my being in Heaven. Nothing appears.

"Check the fridge," Pete suggests.

There they are. "Did you..."

He shakes his head. "All you. Congrats. Nice work."

"Am I moving forward, connecting to the dimensions?"

"Absolutely. You're in charge of what happens next. Won't need my help much longer. But, more data are needed. You willing and ready?"

"Yes. Still want to experience life in ways that were impossible before, such as my kids. I loved watching them grow up, talking to them, seeing them try new things, helping them over rough spots, those kinds of things. But what I'd love to do is understand their world before they could speak. Get into the mind of a one-year-old. Can I do that?"

"Forgotten where you are?"

"No, of course not, but how would it work?"

"Same process as you did for the spider. You can get into their brains and translate what they are experiencing into your adult mind. You'll approximate their experiences into your words, but you'll be sensing their feelings directly. Not quite the same as being them, but close."

"Can I set up what they'll experience?"

"Sure."

"Can it be a place where I am there too?"

"Yes, you'll be in the kid's head, and you won't be messing with time travel's problem of meeting yourself. Want to make it happen on your own?"

"Yes. I'll see you in a while, I hope."

I close my eyes and imagine my son at age twelve months, sitting in the living room playing with his favorite toy, a cardboard box, big enough to hold a bowling ball.

All is dark, then light as Richard and I pull the box off our head. Mommy and Daddy sit on the couch watching and laughing. Dark again, box on head. We're having a great time playing peekaboo. After three times, we get bored. Let's put it on Daddy's head. We have trouble walking and dragging the box and fall twice. We get up and continue forward. Daddy reaches for the box and puts it on his head. Mommy puts it on her head. We want the box back and reach for it. Once we have it, we throw it as far as we can and we don't care where it goes, only that it goes.

A toy car catches our attention. We plop into a crawl and make our way to the toy. Happy. We push the car toward the box and put the box on top of the car. We play peekaboo with the car!

Uh-oh. Daddy left. Where did he go? Is he coming back? Will Mommy leave? We're crying. Mommy picks us up and hugs us. But where is Daddy? Here he is. He has a bottle. Oh boy, nothing is better than a bottle. Drink. Warm. Happy.

Enough, we want down. We want to play with the toy under the box. Let us down. Squirming works. Mommy lets us down. We crawl all over to see what we can find. Here's my hairbrush. Let's brush our hair. Brush. Brush. Brush. Brush. Hey, what does Mommy have? We toddle all the way over to Mommy and fall into her arms. Mommy and Daddy are smiling and clapping.

Mommy talks, about milk, and the bottle. Where is it? It's on her head! We want to put it on our head. She hands us the bottle. We put it on our head but it falls off. We put it on our head again and it falls off again. Where's that other toy with the buttons?

Crawling. There it is. It's upside down and heavy, but we know how to make it right. We turn it right side up. But there's a stick missing. It makes noise when we use the stick. No stick. We bang on it with our hands. Where's the stick? Mommy has the stick. Give it to us! She gives us the stick and we bang on the toy making lots of noise. Mommy and Daddy are talking. We drop the stick. We want to poop. We sit and the poop comes.

There's the box over there. The toy is under the box playing peekaboo. We crawl to the box and turn it over. There's the toy. We throw it. We put the box over our head again. And leave it. Mommy and Daddy are gone. We lift the box off our head. Mommy and Daddy are sitting on the couch. We put the box on our head again and peek underneath to see Mommy and Daddy's legs. We pull off the box and there they are. We throw the box as far as we can and reach for the bottle. A few drinks and we throw the bottle as far as we can. Mommy picks up the bottle. She better give it back to us. She doesn't. She holds the bottle. We want the bottle and crawl to her to demand it back. She talks to us. We want to drink more from the bottle. We beg. Mommy hands us the bottle. She talks more to Daddy and touches our bottom.

The aroma of fresh coffee greets me upon my return to the room. Pete is pouring coffee into a cup on the table but stops. "Or would you prefer warm milk?" He continues to pour while I lift a cheese Danish from the assortment he had laid out. I wonder if I'm packing on pounds. I never asked if the coffee was decaf.

Over the next hour, perhaps longer, I bore Pete by recalling one toddler nuance after another. Most interesting was Richard's simple response to events. He noticed that milk spilled from the thrown bottle, but made no connection between the throw and the milk, observing with no concern and no sense of causality. Events were neutral until they bothered him, like wanting the bottle he just threw.

Although he didn't yet talk using real words, Richard recognized a few words, like bottle. I imagine he would soon ask for one. And it was fascinating to listen to his brain as he played peekaboo. He thought, "Gone, returned, gone, returned" again with no concept of causality. When he looked only at his parents' legs, he knew they were his parents' legs, but didn't know what he would see when he peeked higher. The same thinking was evident with the toy xylophone. Without the mallet, he hit it with his hands, because this toy was supposed to be hit. The muffled sound it made was not connected to hitting with his hands. He saw the mallet and pounded with that because that is what he was taught to do. The louder noise was simply louder noise.

After endless details and three cups of coffee, I finish my child analysis.

"Richard isn't separate from his environment yet," I conclude. "He doesn't comprehend that he affects his surroundings. In psych class in college I learned the 'terrible twos' are a person's first individuation period, with adolescence being the second. Richard was on the cusp of doing that, which I found fascinating to experience in my own son. What precious things they are. If only I had that perception as they were growing up. There was so much more happening than I was aware of. Same for the grandkids. What a missed opportunity. And yet, I was disappointed."

"In your son?"

"Yeah. I didn't get a sense of love from him. I know he was young, but I expected a real connection from him to his dad and mom. We were just objects in his world, nurturing objects, but only objects. I loved him the moment I held him, just minutes after his birth. At least I thought I did. How can you love someone you just met? Was it paternal instinct? Then I got to wondering about Beth. I was attracted to her the first time I saw her, weeks before we formally met. Was that lust that turned into love as I got to know her? Where does love come from?"

"You ask big questions. It might be interesting to note that love for the Father sometimes takes a little time."

"I know. I'll have to mull this one over too. Love seems to be central to life."

"Got something else in mind?"

"I do. Something that occurred this morning, something strange. I think I still have concerns about dying; not sure what they are. It might be because I missed my own dying, being asleep as it happened. I'd like to enter the mind of someone old, knowing there is not much time left."

"Anything we should talk about?"

"Don't think so."

"Okay, while you do more dying, I'll take in a couple of classic TV comedies. I'll be here when you get yourself reanimated."

We're lying on our back, place smells like a hospital; distress and disinfectant. A woman's voice calls, "Mom?"

We're tired. Not much pain right now, mostly deep fatigue and weariness, arms heavy at our sides. We should open our eyes. Our child is calling. Two more breaths. Now we open our eyes. She smiles. What a beautiful child.

"Mom, how are you feeling?"

Too tired to talk. We nod our head and hope to smile.

"Are you hungry?"

We shake our head, no. Didn't she try to feed us earlier? Not hungry. Too tired to eat. Nice to lie quietly. Must connect with her. Her turn to visit. All can't be here.

"Do you want to try to eat?"

We mouth the word "no." Can't be bothered.

"Would you like to hear a little music?"

Wish we could make her feel better; not so helpless. We shake our head again. Must connect; say something.

"You should sit down."

"Yes. I will."

She sits next to the bed and seems to relax. That's good. She has been a wonderful daughter. She is worried. Are we worried? Not much. Not as much as we expected. Losing Harold makes it easier. Not much to live for after losing him. We will be together again, soon. We can't wait. The pain will be gone. The fatigue will be gone. Energy will be back. We will see better, move better. It isn't pleasant crumbling like a worn-out old slipper, bones brittle, muscles almost useless. Pay attention to daughter. Make the effort.

"You should have something to eat. Take mine." We point as well as we can to our untouched lunch tray.

"I'm not hungry. I want to be here with you."

We're sorry she has to be here now. It may happen today. Who do we want to be here? Nobody? In our sleep would be nice. Harold went that way. But hopefully not today. Maybe we'll enjoy more time with the young ones. Hard to believe we're a great grandmother. But if the Lord says it's our time, we're ready. Truth be told, we've been waiting. We'll close our eyes and rest for a moment.

Pain isn't bad; just tired. All the kids visited this week. That was nice. And all but two of the grandkids. That's nice too. They have their lives to live. Old grandma shouldn't be in the way of their young lives. It's good to rest.

Twelve years without Harold is a long time. We're going to be together again. God has been good and will continue to be good. Harold prepared a place for us. He must know we're coming. Married fifty-seven years. Can't complain it wasn't enough, more than most get. We long to touch him.

Need to stay here longer. Daughter needs us for a while. Open our eyes. Easy to keep them closed. Open and talk. Do it.

"Honey, water please."

"Sure, Mom."

She pours half a glass from the pitcher and sticks in a straw, holding the glass and helping us with the straw. Small sip and we shake our head, enough. We nod our appreciation. Too much effort to talk. We are weakening. That is okay. Keep eyes open for a while longer. Look at her, so worried. We're sorry. She wants us to be comfortable. We can't be comfortable; we are weary. Need to shift our legs. Daughter helps. Nod thanks. Close eyes for a moment. Tired. Sleep. Okay to sleep. Good to sleep.

We're sitting in our chairs in the den. Jeopardy is on TV, old Rex at Dad's feet. Silly name for a dog but that's what Harold wanted to call him. Good to remember this; as if it were yesterday. Now we're in the car, the Buick. Sun's out, we're driving along our old street, Beacon Street, looks like toward downtown, out to dinner. How wonderful. Too tired to enjoy it.

"Mother?"

We hear her voice but cannot answer, too far away. Want to sleep. Fatigue falling away. Good to sleep. Comfortable. A light, a nice warm, comforting light in the distance.

"Mom!"

Coming together, coming together. Sleep. We want to sleep. The light dims, darkness closing in. It is time for me to go.

As promised, Pete is waiting when I return.

"Hey Man, what's happening?"

I've heard that voice before on TV, a long time ago.

"You're Maynard G. Krebs, 'The Many Loves of Dobie Gillis.'"

"And the 'G' stands for Walter. Nice guess but I was watching George Carlin as the Hippy Dippy Weatherman. In one skit he did sports. It was classic: 'And now the baseball scores, 4 to 2, 6 to 5, 1 to nothing, 3 to 2 and 6 to 1.' He didn't identify the teams! Hilarious. Back to you. How can I be of service?"

"I think I want to go over today in my head, sort out what it all means. Why don't you come back in the morning and we'll do what else needs to be done, okay?"

"Nobody has to tell me to leave more than once," and out the door he goes.

I pour myself a generous portion of Scotch and sit in one of the chairs ready to reflect. Then it hits me: What am I doing reflecting in this tiny room? I can ponder anywhere in the universe.

I'm above a small and rocky cove on the ocean. At least I assume it's the ocean. I wanted to watch the sunrise in Labrador, Canada. I trusted the system or whatever it is to find what I wanted; a spot to enjoy my drink and watch the sunrise over the wide blue Atlantic. Where I landed is pitch dark and cold. I can see nothing. I'm in the dark, what a great metaphor! Waiting for the light, another great metaphor! Could be the dimensions are more all-knowing and cognizant than I give them credit for. I can see nothing, but oh, I can hear everything: the boom of the surf falling on itself; the crash of waves on rocks; the whoosh as waves slide ashore and the hiss as the water recedes over the sand. The ocean refreshing itself every few seconds.

I recall sitting with Professor Einstein in our aluminum chairs rotating around the earth counter to its spin and a thousand miles above. The light side shining with browns, greens and brilliant blue, the dark side twinkling with a billion lights. Now, above me in the moonless sky are another billion lights, stars, and galaxies beyond counting. A much better setting for reflection than sitting in a chair back in the room.

The wind is cold, but I am dressed for it including a stocking cap. If I snuggle down, I am out of most of the breeze and comfortable. I can hear the ocean and see the stars, feel the wind, sense the wonder of being alive, but I am dead. I am dead, like the woman I died with. I was born, began learning and growing as my son did, lived my life and joined all those who came before, I died. And I'm in Heaven, learning how to be dead.

"What's it all about, Alfie?" I sing that aloud, sounding as thin and off key in Heaven as I did on earth. It was hard enough to figure out life, if I ever did. Now I had to figure out the eternity of being dead. Surprisingly, learning how to be dead seems more important than learning how to live life. At least I'm not afraid of anything at the moment.

Okay. What do we have? Heaven. Seems to be real; I doubt it's a fantastical dream. The Pope entering Heaven. Got that. Hitler entering Heaven. Don't got that. Me, somewhere between the Pope and Hitler closer to the Pope I hope, also entering Heaven. What's missing?

A purpose, again a purpose. What is the purpose of Heaven? I was fine that the universe just is. What's wrong with Heaven being a just is? It works for religious people that Heaven is a reward for faith. That goes out the window when people like Hitler get in. But why not? Should people be doomed forever for making mistakes in life? How much punishment is enough? Is punishment even relevant?

On the other hand, I always held that my life should be purposeful. Lived mine as well as I knew how. Who's to judge? If Hitler is here in Heaven, it would appear that God does not judge. We each could have our own degree of Heaven; not much for the Hitlers, fairly good for people like me, and a grand cathedral-like place for the Pope-like. But again, an eternal fate for what you did over a mere three-score and ten years? Doesn't seem fair. Is life fair? No, it is not. Why should Heaven be fair? I don't know. Seems like Heaven should be fair if any place is. Glad I brought a stiff drink.

I look toward the horizon. There may be a touch of light, not sure. To get a better image, I move my gaze to the left, looking out of the corner of my eyes, using more of the low-light sensing rods. Yes, a touch of light.

And what about babies? Pete said newborns don't

make it to Heaven, not self-aware enough. Hitler makes it but little babies don't? That's not right. Those babies are life, precious, innocent life. I must admit though, my disbelief in Heaven would have doomed them to nothingness too. Hmm.

I need a positive mental shift. I start singing Leonard Cohen's "Hallelujah." But, I'd like to hear K.D. Lang sing the song. So, in the middle of nowhere, in the dark, K.D. Lang sings only to me while I listen and watch the dawn begin. There is an old Buddhist saying, "To truly experience the dawn, look west." That's a good idea if you want to see how sunlight stretches to wake the land and the people. I prefer my sunrises straight up. This one is going to be a beauty and K.D. is knocking "Hallelujah" out of the park, giving me goosebumps.

The pale light is expanding, but with no color yet. The sky is dark, the stars still rule. More diffuse light and a tiny glow of pink. I can see more; flat clouds wait at the horizon. The clouds explode red as gold radiates behind them. Hallelujah indeed. Brighter now, redder while the gold spreads across the horizon, joined by more red and pink in the sky and throughout the clouds.

The magnificent sun appears. First a small dot hardly significant against the brilliance of the clouds and sky. Quickly it takes charge, burning its way upwards. A red cloud, a red smudge, a yellow disk impossible to watch bursting into daylight. Stars disappear in front of me, I don't look behind. I don't care. Dawn is proclaiming that life has returned: The ponderous obligations of the earth dazzled by the unlimited optimism of the sky. All is well. A new day has begun.

Before me, waves crash on the rocks and rush up the beach, spreading the salt and seaweed scent of the sea. Echoes of Hallelujah joins nature's performance. Contentment. This is Heaven.

But what of this place? Only infants and unborn left out? Was there another home for them? I suppose they wouldn't miss anything. This life, they would miss this life.

I worry about the unborn and the too young. And I worry about me. Is Heaven the right place for me?

Sun's up. Scotch glass empty. Time to go.

Day
6

Another's Moccasins

Again, the aroma of coffee when I arrive and this time the sweet smell of bacon too. Pete is in the kitchen assembling bacon, scrambled eggs, raisin toast, hash brown potatoes and a slice of muskmelon.

"Good timing," he says. A quick nod and he returns to assembling breakfast. I sit at the dining table and pour each of us a glass of orange juice.

"What other kind is there in Heaven? By the way, are there separate kinds of Heaven for different people?"

"I'm not sure what you mean."

"I mean, is Heaven custom designed for each person? I always thought if Heaven existed, which I was sure it didn't, but if it did, it would be like the earth, one place for everyone. People would hang out together, doing whatever they wanted and all was cool. No bad guys. No worries. No rain. Just everlasting joy."

"Don't know if my answer is what you're looking for."

"I wouldn't be so sure. You've got a nice place here, as much as I've seen. I like everything so far."

"On earth, that 'one place' you mentioned, do you suppose the world was the same place for everyone?"

"I see what you're saying and agree. Different people see the world differently. Sure. Even East Coast people are different from West Coast people."

"Yes, everyone is different. Some people are smart, some impaired. Some healthy, some with challenges. The world they live in is plural; it's the *worlds* they live in. Plural, plural, and plural. As many worlds as there are people and as many Heavens."

"Is breakfast ready?"

"Just about to put it on the table."

I get up to help. With two trips each, breakfast is on the table and our coffee cups filled. As we sit, I ask one of the questions on my mind.

"Okay. In my version of Heaven, can I include the unborn and the newly born, and whatever other disenfranchised people I find?"

"Sure."

"I thought you said the youngest, too young for self-awareness, didn't work for your purposes, and couldn't get into Heaven."

"Ahh. I see the problem. That's right. Without sufficient self-awareness we cannot design a Heaven for them. But like you, many said, 'I'll take them' and it works out for all."

"I can't tell you how relieved I am to hear that. I almost didn't want to join a club that would accept me as a member and not an innocent newborn baby."

"It's why we do what we do."

At breakfast Pete and I are quieter than usual. I'm not

sure about bringing up my underlying fear and I'm worried Pete can read my mind.

"Penny for your thoughts," he says.

"How close am I getting to gaining the all access freedom ticket into Heaven?"

"You're in Heaven and it's expanding all the time. You've been here five days. This is day six. I trust you'll be where you want to be well within two weeks, most likely in four or five more days."

"What do I do next?"

"Anything."

"I can do whatever I want?"

"Of course."

"I've been struggling to define the right experiences. I don't need to do that?"

"You can do that if you like, if that's where your curiosity takes you. But anything you want to do works."

"If I just want to play, I can do that?"

"Yes."

"If I want to read a book, I can do that?"

"Yes."

"If I wanted to go swimming in the ocean, I could do that?"

"Yes. Yes to everything. You can do anything you want."

"Can I get you more juice?" Pete nods, his mouth full. I get up, open the refrigerator and pull out a now full juice container. The empty one is no longer on the table. I could get used to always having every need met. I pour Pete juice and continue.

"Okay. Another question. What's the difference between where I am now and where I will be?"

"I'm afraid Heaven is the last stop. There isn't any other place to be. You're in Heaven right now. This is it." Pete shrugs his shoulders, appearing genuinely apologetic.

"I assumed we were figuring me out to do something specific to me."

"You're experiencing the fullness of Heaven right now, but not the fullness you will eventually experience."

"Like, 'how high is up?'"

"Right. Sliding scale, no end."

"Heaven evolves as I evolve."

"Well done."

"Hitler will never evolve."

"Nope."

"I'm getting it. Hitler's Heaven is static. It will always be the same. Like the Groundhog Day movie."

"Somewhat like that."

"What about a Pope's Heaven?"

"Same thing. That Heaven was just about completely designed in the Pope's lifetime by what he understood the scriptures to say. Got what he wanted and hoped for."

"What did he want?"

"God's eternal grace; eternal love. And that grows and grows forever."

"Different religions declare their own versions of Heaven."

"Are you asking?"

"Not really. They define different versions. Do they get it?"

"Yes."

"And I don't have one."

"You're in Heaven now."

Without asking, Pete tops off my coffee; punctuating that Heaven provides everything I need.

"Yeah, but I get the impression it's like a beginner's Heaven. Doesn't really count."

"Let's look at it from a different angle. What did you expect to happen after you died?"

"Nothing."

"And you got all this. With your concept of no after-life, you'd be only a memory to family and friends, and that only for a couple of generations."

"Okay. Speaking of that, after breakfast, I'm going on a series of adventures, will probably take all day. Why don't you meet me here for dinner about twenty minutes after I come back and we can debrief. Does that work for you?"

"See you then." Pete leaves with a wave while I clear the table.

I wanted experiences impossible in my risk-adverse life: to battle in world class competition, test the limits of character and courage, and face critical moments in life and history. I was always a middle of the road guy. Never reaching outside my comfort zone. Handled crises when I had to as a dad, but no more than any other parent. My life wore wingtips; now I wanted wings. I will be Michael Jordan, the best basketball player of his time and maybe in history. I pick the 1993 championship series against the Phoenix Suns to play the entire second half with Jordan.

Five minutes left. Game close. We hold the ball; assume we will drive to the basket. Instead, we pass it to the guard on the right and move slowly toward the outside. In a flash we're racing to the hoop. The ball's in the air and we're still running to the basket. Ten feet from the basket we're flying. The ball's coming down and we're going up, both arms raised. A foot and a half above the rim we grab the ball with both hands. We're doing a two-hand jam. "Bam" through the hoop and the net. An in-your-face-disgrace, dunk-o-rama. Most fun I ever had in sports. I am Michael Jordan for half an NBA title game. And we win. Fantastic.

From there I join the U.S. Open Golf Tournament at San Diego's Torrey Pines in 2008, playing the last nine holes with Tiger Woods. We're on the final green facing a twelve-foot putt to tie Rocco Mediate in the top spot. Even at the professional level, the chances of making this putt is maybe one in three and under the circumstances, one heck of a difficult putt. Make the putt and we're in a playoff, miss and it's go home a loser. Tiger and I look it over. We aren't reasoning anything. It's as if we have an animal mind, checking the surroundings for danger, then focusing on our prey, excluding everything but the line of the putt. We see, with certainty, how the ball should curve toward the hole. As we take our stance to putt, the focus shifts to aiming to the point where the ball would begin its curve toward the hole. Hit too hard and it will miss high, hit too soft and it will miss low. The ball has to be struck with exactly the right force. With one hundred percent confidence, we swing the putter into the ball and watch it roll as planned. It tries to sneak out, but topples in the side. "Yes, yes" we know as soon as it drops; tomorrow the tournament play-off would be ours because that's the way it's supposed to be. This little putt was nothing but another step toward our destiny. The confidence we have is something I've never experienced; and the putt was easy to miss. But no hesitation, no concerns, just raw brute conviction it was going in. Absolutely no fear in the strongest mind in sports.

After that I join Kerri Strug in the 1996 Olympics. She was the one who hurt her ankle but remained in the competition. We are last on her team to perform on the vault. If we do poorly, Russia will pass the U. S. and win the all-round competition, as usual. We have to stick our vault, flip and turn in the air and then nail our landing.

We ask the coach if the team needs the vault score and he says we need it. We limp to the start point, pain with each step. Running wouldn't be too bad, pain would be intermittent, but the landing will hurt. The team needs this. One last total effort. Focus only on sticking the vault, only the vault. The landing will take care of itself. Go. Run, run. Leap. Arms out. Vault. Flip. Twist. Extend. Land! Aaaggg. Pain. Hop, hop. Smile at the judges. Coach half carries, half pulls us to the bench. After a time, the judges post the score. 9.712. Enough to beat the Russians. We win. It hurts, but pain means nothing. Only the vault score matters. Stick the landing and the pain would be too late to harm us.

And that is enough for putting myself in the caldron of competition. Elite athletes are elite for a reason. They welcome, even live for the pressure, and feast in the all or none, win or lose arena. I was never comfortable with that. In my job I wanted everyone to win. Next, I want to explore a nagging uncertainty I faced for years. A co-worker's cousin was killed by police in a seemingly innocent situation. Our school district had many minorities. I always wondered how life was different for them. I want to DWB, drive while black. I wonder if I can be in two heads at the same time—a black man and a *white cop*.

We're cruising along a deserted street in a beautiful Cadillac Escalade, black, tinted windows, the works. Real luxury. Late for our boy's baseball game. Eleven. Happy kid. Decent ball player, but we're late, may even miss the start of the game.

We spot the Escalade as it drives by on the cross street. The driver, black, looks like a workingman, out of place driving the luxury SUV. Gotta be an $80,000 vehicle. We pull out to follow him and mull over the situation. Could be innocent, could be part of the recent rash of stolen SUVs. We hate single officer cars; much safer with another officer. Call for backup at this point would be chicken-shit. Handle it ourselves, but be careful. Stop the Escalade, call it in. Carefully approach the driver.

Awww, shit, cop lights in the rear-view mirror. Why would a cop be stopping us? This will make us late. Slow down, pull to the side, stop, window down, hands on wheel. Cop sits in his car like he has all the time in the world and we don't count. Hell man, get your ass moving. He climbs out his cruiser and ambles toward us. Slow like, touches the back end, walking tight to the side. We're waiting man.

"Good afternoon, sir. Are you aware why I stopped you?"

"No idea, officer."

"You were going thirty-seven in a thirty-five zone."

"That's it? You stopped me for going two over the limit?"

"You were over the limit. I stopped you."

"There's no cars around. No pedestrians. Why did you stop me?"

"License and registration please."

"Okay. License is in my wallet, back pocket."

He moves slowly, like he had done this many times before. We realize he could move quickly, too quickly, if he wanted to.

"Registration in the glove box."

When he reaches toward the glove box, he moves even slower, as if to lull us to inattention. We're ready for a gun.

We reach over to the glove box and remove the registration and hand that to the officer.

We watch closely as he pulls out the registration and make sure he closes the glove box.

He looks at the license and at us. He looks at the registration.

The Escalade isn't his. Alarm bells go off in our head.

"Says on the registration you don't own this vehicle."

"That's right, officer. I borrowed it from my uncle. It's his."

"What's his name?"

"Owen Fairchild."

"Where does he live?"

"On Chestnut."

"Number?"

"No idea. It's on the corner, white house."

"Do you have written permission?"

"No, I don't have written permission."

This is beginning to escalate. Have to stop it.

"Don't get snotty with me."

"Sorry officer. I'm late for my kid's ball game."

"I don't care if you're late for your mother's funeral. Keep a lid on the attitude."

"Yes, sir," we say with a brother's slick sarcasm.

Hostility drips out of him.

"How do I know this isn't a stolen vehicle?"

"You can call my uncle."

"Right. Give me the keys please."

"Give you the keys?"

"The keys."

We do. Without a word, the officer, with the keys, registration and license, walks back to his cop car and sits in it for at least five minutes.

We take the keys, license and registration back to the patrol car and search the computer for information. Guy has four priors, two for assault, two for theft. No report the Escalade was stolen, but it probably is. Call for backup, but do your duty. Go back and make this work.

He walks back, looking more suspicious of us than before.

Resistance is rising. Have to keep control.

"Please exit the vehicle, sir."

"Get out?"

"Sir, exit the vehicle."

We get out and the officer moves us to the front of the Escalade and makes us put our hands on the hood.

We guide the gentleman to the front of the vehicle and have him put his hands on the hood.

"Anything sharp in your pockets?"

"You gonna search me?"

"Anything sharp in your pockets?"

"Why you gonna search me?"

"Sir."

"I have a knife in my left front pocket. I used to have my keys in my right front pocket and I used to have my wallet with my license in my right back pocket. That's it."

Stay calm. Stay alert.

The damn officer pats us down. Finds the knife, takes it out and puts it on the hood.

"You always carry a knife?"

"I'm a gardener. I use that knife every day."

"Any weapons in the vehicle?"

"How would I know? I just borrowed it."

"Do I have your permission to search the vehicle?"

"Hell, no. Why don't you give me my ticket now for going two friggin miles an hour over the friggin speed limit and I'll be on my way?"

Keep control.

"Watch the mouth."

The minutes tick away while this clown plays big, bad cop. We could make some of the game if he would just get his ass in gear.

"Officer, just give me the damn ticket."

"We haven't determined ownership of the vehicle."

"My uncle owns it. I borrowed it. Figure the rest out."

"Calm down."

"I'm not calming down. I'm leaving."

We pick up our knife and head toward the driver's door.

He picks up the knife and moves to attack.

The officer jumps back and pulls his gun.

We step to the side and pull out our gun.

We turn toward him.

He lunges before we can stop him. We shoot.

"You shot me. You shot me." And we fall.

I felt both men slipping toward this confrontation unable to stop it. I leave while the police office stands over the driver who is rolling back and forth on the pavement, moaning.

I go from one possible death to hundreds of thousands. I want to find out what President Truman was deliberating when he decided to drop the atomic bomb on Japan. I can't imagine making the decision to kill a quarter of a million innocent people. Couldn't be a larger test of character or a more critical moment in history. Half the victims died instantly, the rest suffered months of pain from radiation burns before dying. Truman was aware this would happen. I spend five or six hours in his head, over a two-year period, beginning in 1943.

What I learn is disheartening. I always believed dropping the bomb was because the Japanese intended to fight to the death, including the civilians in the cities. By dropping two bombs, the Japanese will be forced to surrender, saving hundreds of thousands of civilian and military lives. That's true, but there are other important political reasons. The Soviet Union is making significant gains in Europe and if it joins the effort to defeat Japan in a conventional war, it could increase its influence in Asia. In addition, using the bomb would justify the huge expense of building it. Those people will die so the cost benefit analysis looked good and to push us ahead in our influence race against the Soviet Union.

Truman grasps he is opening Pandora's Box for future political conflicts and possible wars. What would be the ultimate result of his decision: Open the lid for dropping the bomb anytime or shock the world into never using it again? There is no way to tell. He is grim but resolute when he tells the generals to bomb the two cities.

The last thing before coming back is to join President Lincoln writing the Gettysburg Address. I want to experience something grand coming out of something heartbreaking. Hope over tragedy. The President is sitting at a small desk in his study, alone, pen in hand and facing a blank piece of paper. I expected to see him compose on the back of an envelope while on the train from Washington D.C. to Gettysburg, which was the myth. Instead, he begins writing while still in the White House; composing on regular old notepaper. He writes slowly, reflecting the sadness that fills his mind. The war is raging within him as much as in the countryside. After a few sentences he crosses out half the words and continues. The message must honor the dead and begin the rebuilding process even as the war will claim thousands of more lives. He does multiple edits while on the train, and then rewrites the whole thing before putting it into his coat pocket and leaving the train for the speech platform.

Lincoln is somber, soft-spoken. I don't think I've ever seen a sadder man. His clothes reflect his melancholy; jacket sleeves worn at the cuffs and sagging at the elbows.

He sighs, glances at his notes and standing near the front edge of the platform, begins.

Four score and seven years ago our fathers brought forth on this continent a new nation, conceived in liberty, and dedicated to the proposition that all men are created equal. Now we are engaged in a great civil war, testing whether that nation, or any nation so conceived and so dedicated, can long endure. We are met on a great battlefield of that war. We have come to dedicate a portion of that field, as a final resting place for those who here gave their lives that that nation might live. It is altogether fitting and proper that we should do this.

But, in a larger sense, we cannot dedicate, we cannot consecrate, we cannot hallow this ground. The brave men, living and dead, who struggled here, have consecrated it, far above our poor power to add or detract. The world will little note, nor long remember what we say here, but it can never forget what they did here. It is for us the living, rather, to be dedicated here to the unfinished work which they who fought here have thus far so nobly advanced. It is rather for us to be here dedicated to the great task remaining before us—that from these honored dead we take increased devotion to that cause for which they gave the last full measure of devotion—that we here highly resolve that these dead shall not have died in vain—that this nation, under God, shall have a new birth of freedom—and that government of the people, by the people, for the people, shall not perish from the earth.

The applause afterward is polite. It was a long day of speech making. The President raises his hand in thanks and returns to his seat. Although in a somber mood, he is confident his message will be transmitted throughout the North and South, and be heard for what he intended, to begin the peace, to begin the healing, to begin the rebirth of America. That is all I can do, he thought, as I left for home.

Ten hours after I began, I'm back in the room setting the table for dinner. I've conjured simple fish and chips. Cod is my favorite. Baked fries with a sprinkling of olive oil rather than French fried potatoes. Fresh peas. And a nice oaky Chardonnay.

Pete knocks on the door.

"Cocktail first?" I ask. "I know how to keep the food warm."

"Yes, dry martini please. Two olives."

He sits on the couch, I in one of the chairs.

"How were your adventures?"

"Best day ever. I had a list of things to do. Went down the list, did everything. In my day, I wasn't much of an athlete. Experiencing the gifts of arguably the best basketball player of all time was truly a rush. The ease of movement of that guy was phenomenal. It was like being on a thrill ride; I could never guess which way we were going until we were halfway to somewhere else. And Kerri the gymnast was almost in tears with pain, but got taped up and did the vault, knowing when she landed it would be agony. Tiger was really a tiger, an animal that understood he was top of the food chain. Calm and confident when a normal human would be a bag of muscle spasms and brain cramps."

Pete goes through the motions of stretching his arms and back. Then rolls his head around to flex his neck. Maybe he actually was a jock. Then he asks, "Ever wish you had the ability for a sports career?"

"Never did. I was always a bit above average in the games we played and that was good enough for me.

"The other events were sobering, to put it mildly. Driving while black was awful. It ended with the cop shooting the black driver. It was destined. The driver worried from the first moment he saw the police lights. He tried to stay calm, but his fear and anger got the best of him. He wanted to end the confrontation and get to his boy's ballgame. The cop was afraid too and misinterpreted just about everything that happened. Bad for everyone, but mostly for young black males. And their mothers. Mutual mistrust from the beginning. Hard to overcome such a bad situation. I spent time with President Truman as he considered dropping the atomic bomb. I can't tell if dropping the bomb was bad or good; it was the reality. People who wonder if the end justifies the means don't realize there are no ends; life is a series of means. The means must be justified on their own. Never a true end until the final end."

"Did you end the day on a happy note?"

"I did. I was with President Lincoln as he gave the Gettysburg Address. 'That these dead shall not have died in vain.' makes sense of everything, not just the civil war. People live, they work, they rest, they play and they die. They follow their beliefs the best they can. Few endure the horror of war, but none of us, from the most powerful to the weakest, from the famous to the forgotten should die in vain. And we shouldn't have lived in vain either. And there is no one better to commemorate one life than the person who lived it.

"One thing struck me about Jordan, Woods and Presidents Lincoln and Truman. Jordan and Woods were confident, bordering on arrogant. No, they were arrogant, which I guess you have to be when you're competing against others who are equally determined. Lincoln and Truman, who had to prevail on a much bigger state weren't arrogant at all. Just the opposite."

"And the opposite of arrogant is..."

"Character. I wondered about that. Lincoln and Truman weren't trying to win; they were trying to do the right thing. They had a different set of values. Arrogance is an asset for a jock on a small stage against other jocks with only money and bragging rights at stake. Winning is the only goal for them. Arrogance is a tragic fault in a political leader."

"Good lesson. What else did you discover?"

"Biggest lesson for me is that I'm okay. I envied the great athletes, they seemed to be living a larger life than I, which suggests I wasn't taking as many chances or risking as much as I should have. My take-away is that those folks are different, have different gears or something than I do. I wanted to be good at what I did. Wanted to do my best, never needed to be the best. Striving to be the best seems unbalanced to me, compulsive or needy; beating someone to feel good about yourself. My strength was more my character, like the presidents and I liked that. Made my share of mistakes but admitted them, tried to learn from them and never repeat them. I cared about others and did my best to contribute. Even more than before I believe I lived my life well. So many people live lives of unseen opportunities and never blossom."

Pete smiles. "Nothing unseen here. All is as it is meant to be."

"You make it sound like a grand design by someone who cares about people. I thought Heaven was a collection of dimensions."

"Could be. It was already here when I arrived; hard to tell."

"Am I wrong about God?"

"Why don't you ask Jesus?"

Day
7

Sons and Fathers

Last night Pete suggested I take the entire day for myself. He would see me again on day eight. With a second cup of coffee, I sit on the couch the next morning and ponder speaking with Jesus. Raised a Christian, Jesus is the person I should meet. But I don't believe Jesus was holy and equally don't believe anyone else was holy. Perhaps I should seek all the prophets and sons of gods and whatever else they were to get the complete picture.

What would I learn speaking with Jesus? What if he was a charlatan? What if he seemed godlike? Would I convert? What would conversion mean at this late stage? What if this was a final test, Heaven or Hell depending on what I did? Then it hits, worse than before.

A hand around my throat. Choking. Afraid of dying. I'm shaking. This is bad. Why am I shaking? This is bad. Hard to get air.

Stand and walk. Dread is squeezing my throat. Deep breaths. Slow deep breaths. Getting dizzy. Bend over. Too dizzy. Have to sit. Breathe, keep breathing. Slow it down.

Afraid of dying. How can I be afraid of dying? Calming down. Calming down. Slow, even breaths. Believing in God? Is that the price for this new life? No one is saying that. Just the opposite. But I'm afraid, more afraid than I've ever been. I'm at the doorstep of eternity; I'm not up to it. I'm creating my forever; no way of stopping it. No making a mistake. I can't do it.

Calming down. I lean back in the chair. Relax. Storm is over; let's think this through. Pete said it would take a week or two. Not even half done yet. Plenty of time to get comfortable, to understand. Pete is here to help. I'm in Heaven; that alone should take a while to digest. I will be prepared for whatever happens, whenever it happens. I should have faith in the process, in Pete, in what I was and what I will be. Deep breath. I'm okay.

Everything religious is based on faith. I will talk with Jesus.

Jesus is walking through a small village toward a bench in the shade next to the wall of a house. He is darker skinned than I expected, shorter and bulkier, wearing a loose robe and sandals. A few men gather around, begin talking and gesturing. I listen. They are discussing the possibilities of an upcoming trial; I've arrived before Jesus' arrest. The men plead for him to escape. Jesus says little, but it is clear he has no intention of saving himself. There is more discussion. Soon the men move away. Now is the time. I'm nervous. This man, no matter what he is, changed the course of humankind.

I walk toward Jesus and ask if we may sit together for

a moment. He smiles and points to the bench. We begin with a few pleasantries. We chat about the day, the weather, the harvest and other ordinary concerns before I introduce myself as a possible convert. I take a deep breath.

"May I call you Jesus?"

"That is my name."

"I am uncertain. Are you truly the son of God?"

"I am."

"What is your task?"

"I am here to show you the way. You must listen and open your heart."

"I'm afraid of what will happen to you."

Jesus smiles, a sad smile, but with joyous eyes. "Nothing will happen that should not happen. I must do what I have been sent to do; offer my life so you may live."

"I don't understand why you must die."

Jesus smiles again, a grand smile inviting hope and love. "Man has become lost; my suffering will cleanse man's transgressions in the eyes of God. God, through me, will embrace mankind. He will suffer with me as I suffer with you. I will become the bridge to God's love. It is His love that will give everlasting life."

"Why did God create man?"

"Mankind is a manifestation of His eternal love. He needs not man or any thing. Yet, He must express His love and thus created man."

"There is so much suffering in the world. I don't understand why the innocent should be in such pain."

I notice a slight hardening of his eyes. He reaches out and touches my forearm. "The Father gave man life, and man demanded more. He gave a second gift, self-determination. Life was bestowed and a realm in which to live it. Yet man wanted more. Our Father provided another gift, not fate, not consequences, but a world of infinite possibilities. There is good and there is evil, and at the end salvation. Every child enters a world of wonder and potential. Each child unique and each child provided only a temporary home. Life is not to be fair. Life is the chance to be transformed. And life is only the beginning."

He pulls back his hand. We talk for perhaps twenty minutes; until he has to join the men waiting for him. Before leaving he touches my head with the palm of his hand and says, "Accept the love of your Father." At that moment, I feel blessed, a more fulfilling sensation than contentment. I can explain it no other way than his touch was sacred.

I watch him walk with the others until they turn a corner. I'm in a small square containing a spring where the women collect water. Once Jesus is gone, they return and one by one fill earthen jugs. I remain on the bench, wondering what to do next. Was this man the son of God; the earthly representation of God; a messianic psychotic; a well-intentioned commoner? Was I duped by his soft touch? Our meeting felt rushed. I didn't have enough time with Jesus. I was the one who hurried it. He would have given me all the time I wished. What was I afraid of?

Pete may have deliberately left me alone today because I could sure use his wisdom. I am on my own. There was nothing new in my conversation with Jesus. I had heard most of it in Sunday school as a kid. Nice thing was the ideas were consistent, even after two thousand years.

But no proof beyond his touch and who knows what that really was. No documentation for faith, salvation, of Truth beyond truth. Did I expect lightning bolts? An offhand miracle? Signs or no signs, a person is faithful or isn't, simple as that, black or white, right or wrong.

It was easy to dismiss God and Heaven during life; if you didn't believe, there was nothing to lose. Now I know Heaven is real. If this is a test and I fail, I lose. I like it here.

Once the square is empty, I stand and walk toward where I hope a river might be. Good things happen when you're in Heaven and I'm pretty sure I am going in the right direction. Within minutes I'm out of the village and walking along the bank of a shallow stream. It's hot, and there is no cooling breeze. I find a shady spot next to the stream, sit against a tree and watch the water flow by. Why shouldn't everyone be welcome in Heaven? Science and the law understand that people cannot always be held responsible for their behavior; neurologists can even point to malfunctions in specific areas of the brain. Some people aren't given much of a chance. Everyone should be provided the same opportunity but they don't have that on earth so why not let everybody enjoy Heaven? And how many different religions claim to be the only true one? They all can't be right. The stream is telling me we all flow to the same place. All rivers flow to the sea. Is the river right? Do we all flow to the same place?

I wish I had asked Jesus better questions, but I kept stumbling over my words. The right question might lead me to the right answer. Most of the answers included love and faith and not much else. But I can't fault that if the truth depends on love and faith. How much faith can I put into his touch?

On the other hand, accepting a Heaven of multiple dimensions takes a lot of faith too. As Pete said, you can't see or touch them. And this could still be a strange dream and I will soon awake and find myself in my hospital bed about to die and become nothing.

Okay. If I just talked with the son of God and I'm in Heaven, I have to trust there is no Hell and, at worst, I will end up the same place as I expected, nowhere, but more likely I will remain in Heaven forever. Or, there is no God and I'm here in a multi-dimensional Heaven with everyone else. As long as there is no Hell, there is no downside to my belief, or lack thereof. What if directly experiencing His love is supposed to make a believer out of me? Faith through love. Sounds like what religion looks for. And I'm not there yet. I have to get off the fence and decide what I believe.

Like a kid I begin idly throwing stones into the water. Wrestle a stone out of the dirt and fling it into the water. Do that five or six times, then it hits me. I had already talked to Pete about God and being made in God's image and what the multiple dimensions could mean. I had fallen into the same trap everyone seems to. God doesn't have to be a hard-to-believe wise old man living somewhere in the sky. God could be seven thousand dimensions. An all-powerful old man image doesn't have to be a deal breaker. The ancients had to define God as human-like; that's all they could imagine. I can entertain that what they called God, an all-knowing being, is actually a few thousand dimensions of infinite dominion. Jesus could be a few hundred of those dimensions. Did those intelligent design folks accidently get it right?

Need to discuss this with someone, and I know just the someone.

My second apartment after college is paid for by my first teaching job, junior high school science. The place is small and rundown, but within walking distance of the school. My dad is in the living room finishing our joint project, a combination bookcase and stereo system platform. I own a Garrard turntable, Pioneer speakers and a Pioneer amp and receiver; semi-top of the line equipment. The books are college texts I am slowly discarding as I establish myself as something other than a student, although I want to pursue a master's degree in a couple of years.

"Dad. Want a beer?"

"Sounds good. Only one last screw and we're done." He finishes with the screwdriver and returns it to his toolbox, then arches his back relieving the tightness. Dad looks the part of the handyman in his overalls and worn work-boots. Nothing pleases him more than making something work.

I bring two cans from the kitchen just as he lowers himself into one of two beanbag chairs.

"Want chips or anything?"

"Do you have chips?"

"Ah, no."

"Beer's fine."

"Thanks for your help Dad," I say, dropping into the other beanbag. "You're a master at building things. It looks great. Glad we used oak and finished it with stain and varnish before putting it together, made the whole project easier."

"The adjustable shelves will be convenient too. I imagine you'll buy a bigger and better stereo system soon."

"Yup, now I'm working it's bigger and better everything. You want the old one when I do?"

"No thanks. Your mother and I are happy with our console."

"Okay. Got a big life question to ask you."

"Shoot."

"You sent me to Sunday school but I don't recall you or Mom ever going to church, even on Christmas. We didn't say grace. I'm not sure we even had a Bible in the house except for the one I got from attending Sunday school."

"And you're wondering if we're religious."

"Yeah, I am."

"Your mother and I talked about that early in our marriage, and more when you kids were growing up. It was important for you to be exposed, but religion never had a prominent place in our lives. I suppose we believe in God, but don't practice any religion. None of them seemed to be a good fit. Too much punishment; too much worrying about the devil. We did our best to raise you with good morals."

"What do you mean about believing in God but not practicing any religion?"

"We weren't church goers, as you said, and didn't follow the rules and expectations of any religion. Both your mother and I were raised Methodist, but our parents weren't church goers either. I suppose you could call us soft Methodists if there is such a thing."

"What role does God play in your life, just yours, not Mom's?"

Dad looked down for a moment; squirming to get comfortable in the beanbag chair. "Very little, I guess. On occasion, I'll say thanks to God for good fortune or if I avoid something awful. But my view is God doesn't pay much attention to the ups and downs of my personal life."

"What about Heaven and Hell?"

"God doesn't want anyone in Hell. That's mean-spirited and God isn't that way. That's what I meant when I mentioned punishment and the devil. I like the idea of Heaven, but can't imagine not getting bored after about the first 50,000 years."

"So, no Hell, likely God and Heaven?"

"Yeah, that's about it. Sounds like you're trying to figure it out for yourself." My dad struggles out of the beanbag and pulls over a chair from the dinette set. "My back can't take a young man's life style for long. Please continue."

"Can you get into Heaven if you only believe 'God likely?'"

"Maybe not. For the moment, God likely. As I under-stand it, people become more religious as they get older. I'm guessing I'll be the same way. Just hope I time it right. What's your view?"

"God probably not. And I'm working toward becom-ing comfortable with God, not. The way I see it, I bought into religion as a kid, like most people I was indoctrinated before I knew anything. As I grew older, I shifted from doctrine to defining religion only as a hypothesis, one that wasn't supported by any facts. That's where I am now."

"Is this the stumbling toward adulthood of ignorant youth or have you been giving this serious consideration?" My dad studies his can of beer before taking another drink.

"Serious consideration actually. That's why I wanted to pick your brain. I'm a scientist. Faith in an all-powerful invisible being seems a weak reason to run your life a certain way."

"No harm in being religious, as an individual. I've always had the opinion people should do what works for them. That's what drove me to leave mining country and brought me to California. But groupthink can be limiting, even dangerous. We're both aware of how destructive organized beliefs can be against those deemed 'nonbelievers.'"

"Yeah. I'm not looking at the big picture, just wondering about me and my life. Say I get terribly sick and want to end the pain. Laws based on religion would stop me from running my life the way I want to. A god-loving congressman's faith trumps science and limits my decisions about my life? That isn't right."

"Laws should be based on facts."

"Absolutely. Wouldn't you want to end it if you were in great pain?"

"I can't consider that option. There's your mother and you kids. I would fight to the end."

"You wouldn't need to do that for me, but we're straying off the topic. I don't believe in God. Should I, in your opinion?"

My dad sighs, picks up his beer and takes a sip. He's

smart, more than just engineering smart. I remember family evenings when I was a kid. We'd all be watching Milton Berle on television while Dad sat in his chair engrossed in one thick book after another. That's why I want his opinion. He knows more about religion than I do.

"Big question," he says.

"Yes, it is."

"All right, this is what I think. The idea of God is profound, been around in various ways since we became humans. Which makes it suspect. Mythology is a way to comprehend the world when we didn't possess the wherewithal to understand it with facts. Gods come and go as quickly as the cultures that spawned them. Our understanding of God has evolved from the prescience days and you're suggesting that science should replace ancient fables. I get that. Yet our world had to be created by something. Why not a creator?"

"There's always the big bang."

"Yes, but to answer your question, faith has always been a driver for humans, faith that a marriage will work, faith that trying one more time will lead to success. Faith in God seems natural. That being said, a person should follow his heart, wherever that leads. It has worked for me, and your mother."

"The heart circulates blood throughout the body. I should follow my blood stream?"

"You know what I mean." Dad rolls his eyes. He hates it when I lob sarcasm grenades in front of his points. But I have a point too.

"Frankly, I don't know what you mean. Terms like 'heart' just complicate things, but let me respond and you tell me if you agree."

"Fine." Dad sits back in the chair. After another sip of beer, he tilts his head and sweeps his hand forward indicating I should take the floor. I nod my appreciation and begin my discourse.

"As you well know, using the heart as a location of faith or anything else is an idea from ancient civilizations, like the Greeks. The heart, the spleen, the pineal gland, and many other body parts were bestowed special characteristics, with no basis in fact. It was a guess, an assumption, a metaphor, it was something, but it wasn't logical and it is not correct. Our thoughts and feelings are all part of the brain, most likely multiple parts working together. Self-awareness is the same, multiple brain areas working together in a feedback loop. Just because we have only a rudimentary understanding of brain functioning is no reason to revert to superstition and ignorant proclamations."

"Okay. Point made. I was being mentally lazy. To make up for it..." He pops into the kitchen and returns with two more beers. He opens mine with a pssst and hands it down to me.

"Thank you. Then you agree?" I ask.

"Agree. Facts should be the basis of understanding of what life is and should be. You wonder if there is a place for faith."

"That's right. You seem to accept the possibility of God and don't worry about it. Which sounds comforting. I may be over-analyzing. But why accept old ideas just because they came first?"

"I guess my father was more religious than I am, and I am more religious than you. That's the progression, could be that's also progress."

"You're not sure about the existence of God, but you're okay with not being sure. You don't worry about it."

"I figure that if I live a good, moral life, I'll be okay. God isn't a vengeful God. I won't be punished for doing my best."

"You taught me well. Why create people just to punish them if they don't love you? Doesn't make sense. What about a test? Does God test people?"

"Like with Abraham and Isaac, told to sacrifice his son to prove his faith? Why wouldn't God know? Seems unnecessary and small-minded for a God to set up that kind of thing. My guess it is more a manmade story than anything God would do, or need to do."

"True, but you hear things over and over and it's in the Bible. What are you supposed to trust in the Bible?"

"As you said, trust what makes sense and is based on facts. But, God is a comforting concept for many. Something to be said for that."

"Dad, I appreciate you talking to me. This is serious and there aren't many people I can go to or trust as much."

"Son, that's what dads are for. I'm honored you would ask. Can I say one more thing?"

"Of course."

"You're my son and I love you. You've gone to school and worked hard and turned out pretty good. I can't tell you what to do, but I can tell you how. You are a man of character. Trust what feels right to you."

We never met like this when we were alive. Our relationship was close, a good one, but I never asked him about religion. When he died, we had a graveyard service with the immediate family. Didn't even have a minister, just us. Same with my mother when she died. Funny, I have no idea what kind of service, if any, my family had for me. Must be over by now and it had slipped my mind. No sadness in Heaven is true.

I'm not being tested. Dad's right. God wouldn't do that. Pete is trying to help me adjust, help me be content, help me explore my curiosity, and help me eliminate confusion. He's doing a good job. He is not aware of the dread that takes over.

What is my task? Hitler banged straight into Heaven. Could be I'm ready now. Might be why Pete left me alone today. He said a week or two. Today is a week. Tomorrow might be my time. But I'm not ready.

I'm in Heaven. And there is more to Heaven than I've experienced. Everyone can go to Heaven, I like that. There is no Hell. Not sure if we keep our bodies, and even though Pete and I enjoy our meals, it doesn't appear we need them. And I can go anywhere and meet anyone and enter anyone's mind. That seems to be the current state of my Heaven, but not quite the current state of me.

Why haven't I seen Beth? I'm postponing seeing her. I want to see her, but it isn't the desperate need I suffered on my rare business trips, being away from her for only a few days made me desperately homesick. I could see her right this second. See the kids. See the grandkids.

It wouldn't be real. A visit to my family would be too much like watching a video of them living without me. I don't belong there and I don't belong here. That's the struggle. If I belonged in Heaven, as a believer, passing through the pearly gates right off like believers do, then I would know for sure this was the right place for me. I'm dead and I have nothing to replace what being alive was. I don't have Heaven. Heaven should be for believers. Popes go right through and I would guess everyone else does who had faith during life.

The seven thousand dimensions are collecting data to design a custom-made environment to suit my fancy. What good it that? It's like joining a club of one person. I need to move around and clear my head.

What better place for a walk and to ponder life and death than the Na Pali Coast Trail on the island of Kauai in Hawaii; high cliffs, green hills, blue ocean? Doesn't get better than this. I stroll for about an hour, pondering, sitting, looking, strolling, sitting, looking, and pondering.

The third time I sit to ponder in a large grassy area, I decide music would help as I did in Labrador. Unlike Labrador, where I only heard the music, this time I know enough for the singer to appear. My old favorite Israel "Iz" Kamakawiwoʻole and twenty of his friends join me. They dance, arms waving high while Iz strums his ukulele and sings his magical version of "Over the Rainbow" to the delight of everyone. I love songs that celebrate the good of the world and the people in it: The world and the people in it. That's what I'm about on my walk. I gaze on the most beautiful vistas anywhere and think about those I loved, those I admired, those that made the world a better place. My life was about as good a life as anyone had a right to expect. My marriage was terrific, the kids grew up healthy and wise, the grandchildren were a delight and I put together a successful career. I also enjoyed good health until near the end of a long and meaningful life.

Now I find myself in an afterlife. I'm mostly content, interrupted on occasion with that undercurrent of fear. I want to end this day without lingering uncertainty. Trouble is I cannot get a handle on what my fear is about. Belief in God doesn't seem to be an issue unless I am still concerned this is a test. Belief in the afterlife doesn't seem to be an issue because here I am.

I loved life. I loved my life and I loved the people in it. I loved watching the sun rise and the sun set. A cool wind on my cheek was enough to alert me to the joy of existence. A starry sky humbled me and at the same time made me a home in the great cosmos. The ocean, the mountains, even a long drive through the desert asked me to be part of the grand scheme of things.

From what I've learned, the afterlife is more of everything than I could possibly conceive. How can that be bad? Yet, something weighs heavily. Something is scaring me to death.

I hadn't earned my way here, but neither did any of the inhabitants. This is not a reward for living the right life, but only a second home, where they have to take you in. That's different from what I expected. If Heaven existed, it had to be for the devout, not lugs like me. But I am wrong and I accept that. I wonder if the devout feel cheated or if they're even aware of the open-door policy. If they were truly devout though, they couldn't be upset and wouldn't be disappointed.

I sit up on a hill through sunset, although I can't see it from where I am. The sky slowly darkens and then suddenly it's black. The breaking waves seem louder and the air grows damp. Ordinarily I would be on the road by now, but I possess magical powers. I wrap myself in a newly handy blanket and watch the stars appear, first one by one and then in clusters. A newly handy mug of steaming coffee makes staying all the more enjoyable.

I can do anything I want. Is that the problem? There is no challenge, no effort, no purpose. But Pete and I talked about that. We need to talk more. I like the chill in the air; the texture of being. There is no texture in Heaven. I suppose I could ask for Heaven to include random events, like bitter cold sometimes or a touch of the flu. But no Heaven should be the same as earth or whatever planet Heaven's guests inhabited.

Wait. What am I saying? I have been so focused on myself, so unforgivably blind. For billions of poor souls, Heaven is a simple bowl of rice, a shelter for the night, a sore that finally heals. Billions search hours for food or go hungry. My favorite lunch place was a three-minute walk from my office. Countless souls had little or no shelter. My head rested on two pillows every night. I have lost all perspective. I have been so narrow-minded. Thoreau said, "The mass of men lead lives of quiet desperation," and that's true. But that wasn't my experience. I had every advantage and a full, satisfying life. Heaven is for them, not me.

For a universe of men, women and children, Heaven is relief from the daily torments of living. Heaven would be a final and everlasting serenity after death. For me death was the end; for them death would be the beginning, at long last, of a life worth living. Heaven should be comfort and joy, a haven and a rest. I already had that on earth. I didn't need Heaven. My life was complete already.

Meaning in life came from making a contribution, improving the world as well as I could. I can't do that in Heaven; Heaven is already perfect. If I can't contribute anything, there is no meaning. Heaven would be like sucking on a giant teat for eternity.

I shivered, but not from the cool, damp air. Dread smiles as I finally understand it, and what it demands I do. This time, the Grim Reaper will not pay a surprise visit. I will welcome him into my life; maybe we can even become friends. I have to die again.

Day
8

My Blue Heaven

Pete arrives for breakfast as promised. I break the news as we relax in the chairs with coffee afterwards.

"I no longer want to be in Heaven," I tell him.

Pete is as still as a statue, cup halfway to his lips.

"You can't be serious."

"I've decided that Heaven isn't for me and I'd like to respectfully turn down the opportunity."

"Mike, I truly don't understand."

I sigh, a let's-get-it-over-with acceptance of reality. "It was hard to figure out myself but I finally did. When I died, I expected to be dead. I would cease to exist. I was okay with that. Then I arrive here. Total surprise and quite pleasant. Exploring it was fun. To meet the people I did, to experience other people's lives, was fantastic. I have a new appreciation for the wonder of what life is and what it can be. What I don't have is a new appreciation of what being dead is. Dead should mean nothingness, no awareness of anything. Being dead should last forever.

Now I've learned about multiple dimensions allowing continued existence. That's a fine new fact. But here's my conclusion. I lived my life as well as I could. I created personal meaning from the choices I made and by what I did, with the expectation that when I died, it was over. If my life is not over, everything I did has no meaning. The reality of death mandated that I create meaning during my life. Now death is like a fantastic do-over no matter what you lived for or against. I have to be true to myself and to what I believe, which means I must accept that my fate at the end of living is oblivion. I finally realized that and accept it. For me, dead should be dead. I'm ready to be dead again."

Pete is silent. His face is blank, his eyes look down.

"This is quite a surprise."

"Aren't you supposed to be all wise?"

"Just about. What you're saying is you want to continue with what you expected after death, which is nothingness."

I had given it a lot of thought, but feel bad for how Pete is reacting. Yet I have to and want to live and die according to my values. Had God been a compassionate old man living in the sky loving me from afar I might react differently for His sake, but if the afterlife is only a collection of physical dimensions with no soul to them, I must become the decision maker. If I am not true to myself, I am true to nothing. If death isn't meaningful, life isn't meaningful.

"To answer your question, yes, continue with what I expected. I was engaged with my life, doing my best to do it well—I cherished life and what I should do with mine.

No need, no desire to extend it beyond natural boundaries. I was born, I lived, I died, leaving me nothing more to do."

"I understand." Pete nods and is back to his normal happy self.

"Can you make it happen?"

"Of course."

"What do I do?"

"Let me proffer a suggestion first."

"I thought you might have something to say."

"Not to talk you out of ending your afterlife. That is up to you and I support any decision you want to make. Most people trust in a benevolent higher power to make this decision. You want to make it on your own. Yet you haven't experienced all the possibilities and in my opinion you ought to pay the same attention to the ultimate purpose of your afterlife as you did the ultimate purpose of your earthly life. Being dead can be meaningful too."

"O...kay."

"I propose you spend a day in the Heaven your earthly self defined for you."

"You need to explain that."

"Since you were a boy, you worried about the meaning of life and how to live your life well. Over the years, your understanding of an ideal life became defined. You ought to experience it, find out what it's like and determine if it is something you should explore more. The absolute ideal life: Why shouldn't that be Heaven? If you can't enjoy being dead, what good is it?"

"Right. Is it a real Heaven or fantasy Heaven?"

"Oh, it's real. All you're experiencing is real."

"Not sure what 'real' means anymore. My prior life

147

was real, right?"

"Yes."

"Well...then, what made it real? Answer me that."

Pete leans back and laughs. Then he shakes his head in wonder.

"Sometimes, Mike, it seems you ask questions just to see if I can come up with an answer. And of course, I can: The forward passage of time made it real. An act at one point in time affected reality at a later point. One thing makes another thing happen. There is causation."

"I get it. When people did something there were consequences. What happened made a difference and life moved on because of it."

"Yes, same in Heaven. If you end your life here, that's the end of it. You should make sure you make the right decision."

"I agree. Hold on, no I don't. I died in my prior life, but am alive here. Death wasn't permanent. Why should death be permanent here?"

"It isn't. If you die here, it would mean you no longer experience anything. It is the nonexistence you anticipated. You could undo your death, but you wouldn't be aware you had that option. No thoughts or feelings. You would not exist, except within the dimensions."

"Is that like a soul?"

"If you want to think of it that way."

"I will always exist even if I'm not aware of it."

"That's right."

This is getting weird. I get up and pace around the living area; silent as I walk back and forth. I can die and still exist; can exist somewhere and never know it.

"That's creepy," I tell Pete.

"It's a normal state for information, like the information in a computer memory. Nothing happens until you access it. It exists, but is nothing until activated."

"You make having a soul so warm and fuzzy."

"If you want to call it a soul. I thought you would be pleased it's eternal."

This isn't sounding okay. My life was my experience of living and the meaning of it was to contribute. If I don't experience anything or have impact, I'm dead, or may as well be, but in Heaven I continue anyway.

"Do I have impact in Heaven?"

"Same as before, if not more. Heaven isn't artificial. It isn't a fantasy, it isn't playacting and it isn't an amusement park peopled by robots or actors. It's hard to understand, which is why I suggested you experience your ideal-life Heaven."

"Okay. Count me in."

"When you're done with your pacing, walk through the door."

Our house is made of wood and local stone to fit the look of the cliff side. The slope is gentle and the house itself is in the middle of about a third of an acre of level land perched fifty feet above the ocean on the central California coast. Except for a small sandy beach, the coast is rocks continually pounded by waves. It's plenty large for Beth and me, and our family when they visit. I enjoy many favorite spots: my library with the view, the large living room with floor to ceiling windows, the patio in back where you can almost feel the waves hit and the bedroom, also with the ocean view. Skylights bring the sun's brightness into the entire house. There is not one thing I would change even if I had fifty-million dollars.

Our touristy little town, Carmel, is less than half a mile walk. My second favorite golf course, Pebble Beach, is only a few miles away and my favorite, Cypress Point, just a mile beyond that. I don't play much and I'm lousy, but nothing beats a round of golf with my friends, which is set for next week.

At the moment, I'm sitting on the patio. It's about eight o'clock in the morning. The sun is up, sparkling off the rippling water. The breeze is gentle and cool, just how I like it. Sixty yards out two sea otters float on their backs in the swell. Sea lions bark a short distance away.

On the agenda today is a visit to a youth center. Tuesday there is a school board meeting. We're tackling improving science education for middle school kids, a favorite topic of mine.

Beth is somewhere in the house, no idea where. She is probably putting together the menu for this afternoon's family barbeque. She organizes everything; I'm the griller. I do the easy part. The kids and grandkids live close. Our parents are still alive and live close enough and our sibs visit as often as we like. Everyone usually comes here because they like the house and the setting, and it's about an equal travel distance for everyone. Today we're celebrating nothing but the joy of being family. But it's just the big kids and the little kids, not the old folks. We want extra time with the grandkids to spoil them rotten as much as we can.

I learned a lot when I fell for Beth. I had no idea that love was overpowering; thinking of her all the time, wanting only to be with her. Even as we struggled in the early days, love made everything okay. Then kids arrived. I had no idea they would be overpowering too: Holding a newborn, changing a fussy twelve-month-old, enjoying a conversation with the same kid only a few months later. First day of school, first evening of homework, it never stopped being a challenge and a joy. No way could it be better. Then grandkids arrived and I was bowled over again. They were part of me once removed; more exotic, and somehow more responsibility. All were brilliant, all were beautiful no matter how smart they were or how they might look to others. Beth and I focused all our energy on them, pacing ourselves and the visits for optimal impact and fun. Give them back, recharge and reach for them again.

"Where are you, Grandpa?"

"Hi honey. Where have you been?"

"Getting ready. I'm manning the co-op this morning."

"Which one?"

"The highbrow one on Ocean."

"I'll be home about twelve-thirty or one o'clock. Will you be back by then?"

"Should be. Shift ends at noon, but I'm not sure when I'll get back. If I'm not here, start the prep without me. Remember, only the kids and grandkids. Don't make enough for an army."

She walks over and the most beautiful woman in the world kisses me goodbye on my forehead.

"Have a good time," she says.

After getting ready for the youth center class, I make

my way to the garage. There, sheltered as it should be, my grand steed awaits, a Bentley Mulsanne. I splurged getting it, but it was a great decision. I love that car. What a great sound system, like being in the middle of a concert hall. The head-bobbing beat of the Beatles or Rolling Stones makes me young again. Then look out for the deep throb of soul, namely Aretha Franklin. And B.B. King; nothing sounds better than B.B. King. Except Willie Nelson singing "On the Road Again." I love driving to that one.

This morning I'm subbing for my friend Carlos at the Salinas Youth Center. The forty-minute drive allows me time to consider the needs of the kids I will be seeing. There should be five showing up for the class designed to help boost academic achievement for those that are struggling.

I'm most worried about Angelina, the youngest in the class. She's fourteen but looks twenty and is gorgeous. Unless she learns how to handle the attention of boys and probably a few men, she may end up pregnant and be derailed, never to regain any headway in life. Jose is also a problem and one I don't handle well. The few times I've conducted the class I get irritated at the kid. He's short and fat; a blob. There is no energy, no drive toward anything. But he never misses a class which I hope means something. Ricardo is okay, way behind but okay. His parents are new immigrants and he is busy learning English and figuring out how to attend school and do homework. With support he will be fine. Elena is a problem and an opportunity if we can figure out how to support her. She's the oldest of six siblings and takes care of them and the house while her mother works two jobs. The father took off a year ago. Mateo has only a few months left in school but we're hoping we can help him stay for another year. He is not prepared, knows it, but is trapped in a life that demands he earns a paycheck.

We spend our two hours together reviewing homework assignments and clarifying questions and concepts. Jose, the lump, isn't bad today. He helps Angelina with her math homework, interested in figures but not hers. Could be he is simply a nerd and I need to take more time understanding his interests.

At the end of class I ask my traditional two questions: what went well today and what can be improved for next time. What went well was everyone saying they learned something. What can be improved? "Nothing," they yell together. I love subbing for Carlos; just enough teaching to feel good and not so much to burden my schedule. I love having the chance to affect someone's life in a positive way.

On the drive home I listen to Fleetwood Mac, loud. The beat has me driving too fast. Beth isn't home when I arrive. I busy myself putting together the condiments and supplies for the barbeque. Once that is done, I form the hamburger patties. My secret is twenty percent fat augmented with pork and to loosely pack them to form air pockets. That allows more even heating. I make ten and store them in the cooler outside next to all the hotdogs my brood could manage. I fill the barbeque with charcoal and wood chips and light her up. A quick reconnaissance confirms everything is done that can be done until receiving further orders from the boss. I make an iced tea and carry it to the patio. The warm sun and my lounge chair await.

This is my favorite spot. The flagstone patio is large, expansive enough to hold a party of thirty or forty people. I hate it when guests must crowd together or stand off the patio itself. We don't hold many parties, but it makes me a rich man to relax and view a large expanse.

Although I don't see any now, one of my favorite pastimes is to watch container ships off in the distance on their way to exotic faraway ports like Shanghai or Rio de Janeiro. I'm a hopeless non-seafaring romantic. I also like to see the giant private yachts that will dock in Monterey. How people can spend all that money and use these floating palaces only a few times a year is beyond me. Give me a large patio, a water view and an iced tea and I'm good.

"I'm home."

"On the patio."

Beth pushes through the French doors from the living room and joins me. She perches on the arm of the chair next to me, clearly indicating she will not join me because she has things to do, probably things I should have been doing. Before saying anything, she looks me up and down.

"I see you showered, that's good. Ratty tennis shoes, looks like tide pooling is on the agenda Cargo shorts. Okay. Hawaiian shirt. Fascinating taste. Well, had a great time at the co-op this morning. Lots of tourists and lots of sales. Two of mine."

"Great. Which ones?"

"The one I really liked, with the rock with the wave crashing against it. A cliché, but I did a good job of it and the other was the flock of sandpipers strolling along the shore."

"Did they appreciate them as much as you hoped?"

"Oh, yes, that makes all the difference, doesn't it? How did your class go?"

"Everyone made progress."

"Well, we're a family of winners. I see you've set things up. Did you make the burgers?"

"Yep, everything's done. Awaiting your instructions."

"I'll get changed and let you know. You take care of relaxing in the sun."

So I do. Must have dozed. First thing I realize is it's about time for the family to arrive and I haven't been asked to do anything more. I take the last sips of my now watery iced tea and gaze out to the horizon. Ah, contentment thy name is ocean. And sky. And the smoky aroma of the barbeque. And the smell of pine. And...and the sound of grandchildren pushing through the door.

"Grandpa." The most joyous sound known to humankind. I'm swarmed by skinny arms and enthusiasm. I can't even get up. All four are jumping and pushing and grabbing and squealing.

"All right, all right. Let me get up so I can give you a hug and a kiss."

They line up as I taught them, tall to short. A hug and a kiss to each welcomes them to Grandma and Grandpa's house. I try not to make it too formal or structured, but Beth insists we exert control and she's right. They scatter to play while I go inside to greet the old kids.

The daughter and her husband, and the son and his wife are in the kitchen talking with Beth.

"Hi everyone." More hugs. I continue. "Any news from the outside world?"

Beth answers. "We were just talking about the election; what a surprise it was."

"Not to me," our son says. "He was a long shot, but he also was the best candidate."

One of the things, out of many, that I love about my family is that no one takes the bait. We've got opinions, but don't need to share them or worse, expect people who have other views to listen to us. My daughter-in-law is a saint to put up with the misguided ideas spouting from her husband every day or at least at family gatherings.

"Son," I put my hand on his shoulder, "come tell us in six months how you see things and I'll be happy to fix you a stiff drink with which to drown your sorrows. Speaking of drinks, I'm taking orders for service on the patio."

I take the orders. The men file to the back. The women stay in the kitchen. Once settled in, I ask the traditional question, "How's work?"

Both boys say, "Fine."

I say, "Got a big problem. Could use your help." I love it that both lean forward to give me their attention.

"I've been working on improving the middle school science curriculum. More and more girls seem to be interested, but few stay in the sciences into high school and college and that is a waste of brainpower."

"You should ask the ladies," is the first reply and it's true, but I want to start with the male point of view. In our ignorance, we discuss how middle school girls get distracted by more pressing things like boys and makeup. We guys continue to problem solve from our inadequate understanding of what is really happening. Then the ladies come out, join the discussion and set us straight. What a family.

After the maestro of the grill has cooked hamburgers and hotdogs to perfection, when the potato chips have disappeared, the dip bowl has been scrapped clean, and after the last juicy slice of watermelon is only a rind, I take the kids to the tide pools. I carry the youngest, he's only three. The five-year-old girl, the six-year-old boy, and the ten-year-old girl rush ahead. They've learned that tide pools are homes to the animals and we are not to disturb them. That's why we don't take buckets and implements of destruction. We are to look and rarely touch. The kids skip their way down the cement and stone steps, put in expressly for this walk to the beach. At low tide, dozens of tide pools wait to be explored. The older kids surround one by the time we arrive.

"What have we here?" I ask, bending down and releasing the kid, but keeping a close watch.

"A starfish."

"Anemones."

"Mussels."

The kids know their stuff. We explore each tide pool as a team, pointing out what we see to each other. Each time we look, we're searching for the rarest of finds, hermit crabs. Somehow, they must sense we're coming and skedaddle out of the way. Today we find two, and watch in fascination as they clamber along the bottom of one pool, up the sides and over to a second pool. I whisper to the kids they're doing a great job of looking without disturbing. I don't need to whisper, but it makes the expedition more mysterious. After inspecting every pool, we return to the small beach to make the greatest sandcastle in the history of the world. My intent is to get the kids so dirty their moms will go into shock. Half an hour in the wet sand does the trick. Before we head back, I remind the kids that the ocean will reclaim the beach later that night and wash away the castle. I also remind them that next time we'll build an even bigger one.

Upon our return, the moms reach for their filthy children moaning when they see the head to toe dirt, probably for my benefit since both brought the kids changes of clothes. When the kids return, fresh and ready to go again, I suggest we start a fire in the fire pit. The sky is preparing for sundown; the perfect time to roast marshmallows, even make s'mores if the moms help. And, of course, they do. We men sit in our chairs sipping our favorite after hamburger drinks, mine is Scotch, and watch the kids try to singe their marshmallows without turning them into fireballs.

How did I get so lucky? The love of my life loves me back. We raised two great kids who think we're great, for the most part, too. Their spouses treat us with what seems to be genuine love. And our grandkids are the greatest huggers in the world. The biggest challenge is to treat the ten-year-old as a kid when she wants and a young adult when she wants that. She is teaching me in her own way how to keep up with a child who doubles in complexity every time I see her. And the three-year-old. Watching him develop reminds me how precious and how swift life is.

Too soon it's hugs all around and they're gone. After I bring in what was outside for the barbeque, Beth insists she will clean up the kitchen and orders me outside again, this time with a sweater. I'm too proud to take a blanket, but next time I will, my legs are cold as soon as I reach the chair. The sun had set not too long before I sit myself. The pounding of the surf against the rocks is hypnotic. I wait until a few stars appear before I go back into the house. I can see the sky from the warmth of inside if that's what I want. Beth is still in the kitchen. I plop into my favorite chair, turn on the table lamp and peruse the magazines on the side table. There is a book too; strangest novel I've ever read. I am halfway through *Flatland*, by a fellow named Edwin Abbott. It was published in 1884 and is about people who live in a two-dimensional world. In this world, women are shaped like lines, men in shapes like squares and octagons all the way to near circles. The more circle-like, the higher the status. Because women are sharp and can puncture men, all women must enter homes through a women's only entrance. Supposedly the book was a wicked satire of Victorian mores. When the main character learns about three dimensions and tries to tell others, he is thrown in jail. That speaks to what happens today when the need to make changes comes up, one side is right and the other belongs in jail.

But, the new issue of "Scientific American" beckons. I want to read more about one of my favorite topics, black holes. How can such monsters exist and what connection is there with creating wormholes? This issue has an article on black holes and another one on string theory. I like that "Scientific American" covers the science well, but is also understandable by a semi-science person such as myself. My educational background is now considered ancient.

I choose the magazine over the book. I don't want to finish it yet and it's a short book. The article on black holes it is. It's slow going. I stumble over a few simple equations that are not simple enough. But with extra concentration, I'm able to make sense of what the author is teaching me. I'm becoming well versed in black holes and about ready to take a deep dive into string theory.

The kitchen light goes off and Beth comes into the living room.

"Honey I'm going to bed. By the way, I bought a new nightgown. Might be too young a style; shows more of me than I probably should. See you in bed. Don't take too long."

I finish reading the paragraph, put down the magazine, turn out the light and scamper into the bedroom.

It's good to be me.

Day
9

Truly Heavenly

Pete and I stretch out on the pool lounge chairs. A carafe of coffee and a box of donuts wait on the table between us.

"Okay," he says. "Tell me about yesterday."

"Great day. First, I didn't realize I was in Heaven. It seemed normal. Driving a Bentley was the same as driving a Ford. Except it wasn't. That car was fantastic. Smooth as melting butter on the road. The leather seat was huge, as big as any recliner. The sound system powered a dozen speakers and the trunk could have held a small dinner party.

The house was perfect, right on the ocean; big, stylish, yet not ostentatious. Must have cost thirty or forty million dollars. And it's hard to imagine such a house within walking distance of central Carmel, but it was. The giant patio was something I've always wanted. I would be happy to sit there looking at the water forever."

"You think?"

"I get what you're saying."

"Aren't you worried you'd get bored living in that home for twenty-million, billion years?"

"That's what I'm wondering."

"Would it be possible to get bored in Heaven?"

"By definition, no. Heaven is supposed to be a great place. But how is it possible?"

"You owned a Bentley. You lived in a forty-million-dollar house in Carmel on a Superintendent of Schools' salary. How is that possible?"

"That's not the same thing."

"Why not?"

"Because a car is a thing; a house is a thing. Me being bored is me, my perception of reality. And if reality doesn't change for a million years, I'd get bored."

"Okay. Let me explain more about how Heaven works. That day you had yesterday, was it a great day?"

"The best day possible."

"Good. Were you concerned about the day before or the day after?"

"I was concerned about solving problems, but wasn't focused on the day before or the day after."

"You were in the moment, so to speak. That's why you would never be bored. In Heaven, you focus only on what you are doing, not that you've done it before or you will do it again. You're doing whatever it is now and it's great."

"It's like I wouldn't remember things?"

"Something like that. You would have a history and you would anticipate tomorrow, but you wouldn't be accumulating memories as you did in life."

"Every time I did something it would be the first time?"

"No. Like your teaching; you taught the class before and had a memory of teaching it, but it wasn't as if you had taught it a million times and were tired of it, even if you did."

"There is something wrong with that, but I'm not sure what."

"You're still conceiving time in the old way, that life has to advance, make progress toward something and also leave a wake, memories. Heaven isn't like that. Heaven is chocolate pudding without having to eat your lima beans first. You've reached the goal, now you can enjoy it."

"Yesterday was my ideal life. Relax and enjoy it."

"Yup. An ideal life and a real life and a Heavenly life all in one."

"My parents would always be there, my grandkids would always be grandkids, young enough to treat me like I'm a wise old man."

"It's better than that."

"Better than my ideal life?"

"You can live multiple ideal lives. You can live a life as an eighty-year-old, as a ten-year-old, as somebody else. It's all what you want. The key is that your existence, as you experience it, is complete, and wonderful, one moment at a time."

"I get the problem. If I can change what I want, I must be aware of what I'm doing. Then I'd realize what I'm doing is no longer satisfying and I would want a change."

"That's the beauty of it. Whatever you're doing is perfect. You will be content and satisfied every day. You won't want anything to change, but if you did, it would change. But you won't."

"What if I wanted to find out how my grandchildren turn out?"

"You won't. But if you did, you could."

"If I wanted it to, how would it happen?"

"It would simply happen, like you had a Bentley. That's why all the data points, to make everything that needs to happen, happen."

We're quiet for a while as I let that sink in and I take the opportunity to reach for a cream filled donut; one of my favorite eating indulgences is to alternate a bite of donut and a sip of coffee. I stuff my face and ponder too. It doesn't seem possible to be self-aware and not be bored or want to time travel to explore the future of my family. On the other hand, if my total awareness is of one moment, my self-awareness would be limited to one moment too. I wouldn't worry about the future. In Heaven, I might wonder about it, but not worry. In fact, that's probably how it works.

"Another question."

"Shoot."

"Was that Heaven specifically for me?"

"Yes."

"When Beth dies and she is experiencing a perfect life Heaven, would it be different?"

"Yes."

"So everybody who is experiencing a perfect life Heaven would be experiencing a different Heaven, even though many of the people in it will be the same people; like my Heaven has a Beth and her different Heaven has a Mike."

"Hope so."

"One more. When I was experiencing working on problems, like my committee work, was I trying to solve real problems?"

"Yes, they were real problems."

"Last question, I think. That perfect life Heaven was designed for me. Was my prior life designed for me?"

"No. You were created by chance and entered a world where anything could happen."

It's beginning to make sense. In life, my contribution was needed; the world needed something from me to make it a better place. My perfect life Heaven was for a place for me to make a contribution, but only because that is one of my needs.

"Okay, Pete. Things are beginning to make sense. But, if I decide to end things later, I want to make sure I can. Can I?"

"End yourself at a later date?"

"Yes."

"Yes."

"Interesting. I think you just proved God doesn't exist. He would never allow that."

Pete laughs, leans toward me, and points his finger at my nose. I flinch. He isn't usually demonstrative.

"I'm sorry," he says, leaning back, "but it's funny. You're already dead. You can't commit suicide. What you do next is fine with everyone no matter who or what it is. No double jeopardy here."

"Oh, yeah. I'm already dead. How could I forget that?" Not much else to say on that matter.

"Are you ready for your next Heavenly experience?"

"Yes. Except this time, may I keep self-awareness? I want to experience it and also evaluate it at the same time. I wasn't able to do that yesterday."

"Of course. I hope you find this Heaven fascinating. Remember, you subconsciously designed this one based on your imagination of a religious Heaven. This was you, designing Heaven as if you were God."

"Yeah, I'm curious to find out what kind of god I would make. Well, what kind of celestial home I would make for my people."

"Ready?"

"Yes."

"Walk through the door, just like yesterday."

"You're such a drama freak," I tell him and wave like he does as I walk through the door.

God must have un-formed the Heavens and the earth. There is no horizon, no land, no sky, only a blue-green glow everywhere. It isn't transparent, but it isn't dense like a cloud either. I'm alone in it, whatever it is. More startling is my mood. It's similar to when I had IV Valium prior to surgery. Then I was giddy; now I'm euphoric. Not a take-off-my-clothes-and-run-around-naked euphoric, but a comfortable, I-should-be-this-way-all-the-time euphoric. I have a body, but it doesn't feel like a body. I am weightless, but not floating.

I turn in a circle. I jump, but instead of leaping, now I float. Not sure how high, there are no reference points. I may be floating miles high or be still, I can't tell. I lean to the left. Can't sense if I moved or not. Same thing leaning right. No idea if I did or not. I fall backward. No idea what happened, if anything. This is like floating in a giant blue-green egg. Yet it isn't scary or claustrophobic. I bring my knees to my chest and don't fall. I stand on one leg without wobbling. I can walk, but I'm not sure if I'm making headway. I can sit, but am sitting on nothing. I bend forward from the waist and bring up my legs behind me. I should be prone, face down, but feel as if I'm still upright. I twirl as ice skaters do. That works fine. I stop.

Two figures appear out of the ether, perhaps a hundred yards away. They come toward me, either walking or floating, I'm not sure. Oh gosh, it's my parents in all their 1950s glory. My mother is wearing a dress that flows outward from the waist, high heel shoes, a string of pearls and white gloves. My dad is in his Convair engineer's uniform, short sleeved white shirt, narrow tie with tie clasp and his black plastic framed glasses. I'm surprised he isn't wearing white socks. They each look about forty-years old. My mom reaches me first, enveloping me in the grandest hug. Then it's my dad's turn. He wasn't a hugger before, but has learned how. It's the best. We sit in the new way, on nothing.

"We're glad to see you and are so proud of you," my mother says.

"Yes, son. We're happy you're here."

"And I'm, I'm astounded. How are you?" That just came out. Of course they're great; they're in Heaven for crying out loud.

"We're fine," my mother answers. "We've been busy, there is much to do."

"What is it you do?"

My father answers. "Oh, a little of this and a little of that. You know, everything. There is everything to do here."

"Would you like a tour?" Mom asks.

"Yes."

With that, we get up and I notice the ether has transformed into a five-story building, all glass and steel. Dozens of people walk/float in and out of the openings, there are no doors.

"This is one of our centers," my dad explains. "It's where we get together to do what needs to be done."

"What kinds of things need to be done?"

"Everything," my mother says.

As we approach the opening, no one says anything, but I sense the exchange of greetings. Warmth and friendliness radiate outward and toward each of us. Once inside, we make our way to a table. Two women of indeterminate age sit behind it, but not on chairs. Both smile as we approach.

"How may we help you folks today?"

My dad puts his arm over my shoulder, something he hadn't done before in my memory and tells them I am their son, newly arrived and I am curious about where I find myself.

"Wonderful," the second woman says. "Why don't you go to the third floor and meet with Donna. She is the one to start you on the right foot."

We walk/float up a ramp to Donna on the third floor. She too is behind a desk, and sits, not on a chair. My dad explains the situation to her.

My mother chimes in.

"We would be happy to show him around. Are there certain things we should do?"

"I don't think so. Anything particular you'd like to see or do, Mike?" Donna asks.

"You know my name."

"Yes. And I know your parents."

"Are there places I should visit?"

"You'd like to meet God, wouldn't you?"

Ah. Hmm. "Yes, yes, meet God, yes."

"We wanted to teach him, but we were terrible examples. None of us expected what happens. It must be quite a shock to him," my dad looks at me, "to arrive in the afterlife."

"It was for us too," my mother adds.

Donna has a few ideas that make sense to my parents and seem okay to me. Meeting God is first on the agenda. No one said anything about an appointment, but I hope for a little delay to get comfortable about this unnerving opportunity. I suggest lunch. My parents laugh. They haven't eaten in decades, but would eat with me if I wanted that. How about coffee? No sooner suggested than the glass and steel building reassembles into a Starbucks.

We sit at a table, this one with real seats while my dad collects three cups of today's special at the counter. I ask my mother about the woman serving my dad.

"Yes, she's real. She's like us. That's what we all do, when there is a need, one of us meets it. Thanks, Sharon." My mother waves to the woman, who waves back.

"Same with the women back at the building?"

"The building? Oh, I forgot there was a building. That was for you. No need for buildings here. There is nothing we need to be sheltered from."

"Where do you sleep?"

"We don't. No need for sleep either."

"You're awake twenty-four seven?"

"There is no twenty-four and no seven."

"You're awake doing things all the time."

"There is no time."

"Do you and Dad hang out together?"

"No. I haven't seen him in a long time. So to speak."

"I don't understand."

"We're together for you."

"Like the buildings and coffee are for me?"

"Yes."

"I don't understand why you and dad aren't together. You didn't divorce while in Heaven, did you?"

"Oh no," she laughs. "It's nothing like that. No physical bodies in Heaven. We don't need them. Our bodies right now make it easier for you."

No bodies I can accept, but I don't understand the mechanics of it. If you're not a physical body, what are you and what boundaries are there? I want to mull that over. Dad brings the coffees to our table.

"Hey Dad, Mom and I were talking about you guys not having bodies. Does that mean there aren't other physical things, like trees, mountains..."

He passes each of us a paper cup of coffee, no lids. I take a quick sip, perfect drinking temperature and an out of this world flavor. Best coffee I have tasted.

"That's right. There is nothing here."

"But things could be here if you wanted them."

"Sure, anything. But we don't want anything."

"And you and Mom don't connect with each other often?"

Dad looks over to Mom. Then looks back at me.

"She sure is a beauty, isn't she?"

"Just like I remembered. It's great seeing you guys."

"We don't connect with each other, son," my dad continues, "because we don't need to. There is a collective consciousness. Everyone is part of the whole. We don't have bodies or any needs, we don't take up space, we're all together with God. One mind, one heart, one soul; however you want to describe it."

"Ah, when you died, you become one with God and everyone."

"That's right."

"I don't recall you two being big believers."

"We weren't disbelievers," my mom says. "We didn't attend church and didn't pray much. Your father and I didn't pay a lot of attention to religion, but deep down we both had faith. Seems like we believed enough and lived a life good enough to be granted our home in Heaven."

"You spend all your time in this collective consciousness?"

"Yes," they both answer at the same time.

"And you don't do anything?"

"Right, until needed."

I would like to reflect on that too. I change the subject to the one that is making me anxious.

"When do I meet God?"

"Well," my dad says. "There are two ways to do that. We can take you somewhere where you can meet him, but like us he doesn't have a body. What you'd be visiting is a representation of God. You'd probably see an old man with a beard. Even calling God a 'He' is only a convention. Or, you can join the collective consciousness and experience everything the same way we do."

"I'd like to do both."

The coffee shop disappears and is replaced with a classic Greek edifice about forty-yards away.

"Go up the steps," my mother says. "Go through the entrance and God will be waiting. You don't do anything special. God will guide you, just follow His lead."

I walk/float up the steps and between massive marble columns. Thirty-foot high doors slowly swing open as I approach. Inside a room the size of an airplane hangar, in the middle, on a throne at floor level, sits an old man with a white beard. He is wearing a loose robe and is barefoot; of course God wouldn't need sandals or shoes and socks. He motions with his hand for me to come forward. I do and stop in front of him with my hands clasped. I should be shaking to my bones meeting God. But I'm not, I'm meeting God and I am content, and loved.

"I understand you wanted to meet me." His voice is gentle.

"Yes, sir. I very much wanted to meet you."

"And what is your impression?"

"I have so many questions."

"Ask. I will answer as well as I can."

"You exist?"

"I exist."

"In what way?"

"In all ways."

"Have you always existed?"

"I have."

"Where is Heaven?"

At that He laughs. God... *laughed*.

"Heaven is everywhere."

"If I make it to Heaven, will I understand every-thing?"

"You've made it to Heaven and you will understand everything."

"What about mankind being made in your image?"

"That is true, but has been misunderstood. Man was made in my image in regard to love, compassion, the joy of life, not the simple manifestation of the body. The body is unimportant."

"Made in your image..."

"Is in the greater spiritual realm which is all that is important. The physical body is only a temporary home. Heaven is the true home for humankind. We are all one here."

"Why did you create us?"

"You have lived the answer. Love must be expressed to have meaning."

I look at him, taking a good look. He doesn't appear godlike, but He sure doesn't look ordinary either. I don't need to hear any more. Trying to represent all humankind, I say, "Thank you."

God rises from the chair, turns and walks/floats to-ward the back of the room and disappears. I exit the room toward the front, go through the giant doors, between the pillars and down the steps toward my parents. Halfway there I turn toward the building and, of course, it's gone.

"That was something. I'm glad I met him. It was what

I imagined, which seems silly to say, but seeing Him was fantastic. He answered all my questions. Although I still don't understand the God, Jesus and the Holy Spirit combination."

"You'll find it doesn't matter," my dad says. "We're all one here."

"That's what God said."

"It's true," my mother adds. "And it's beautiful."

"How do I join the collective consciousness?"

"Why don't we go to a park, sit on a bench together and we'll ease you into the experience," my dad suggests.

We walk/float to a wooden park bench which sits under a large oak tree and faces a small pond. Across the pond are more trees.

"Sit here," instructs my dad. "Take in all that is around you."

A gentle breeze ruffles the dark pond water. The same breeze rustles the leaves across the pond and above our heads. Between us and the pond is a narrow dirt path.

"Listen to the sounds."

I listen. I'm first aware of the birds chirping in the tree above us and in the trees across the pond. Small waves slap against the shore.

"What do you feel?"

The breeze against my face. The firmness of the bench. The euphoria of being in Heaven.

"Close your eyes and let it all come together."

I close my eyes, imagining the trees and the pond, my parents, the bench, the breeze, hearing the birds and the leaves. I picture an artist painting this scene. And watch as she applies paint to the canvas. Violin music begins in the background. Then voices, not distinct enough to catch words, just the murmur of voices. Euphoria increases. I wonder about meditation and hypnosis. Those disruptive thoughts merge with newly formed colors, pinks, blues, greens, all pastels. The murmurs increase a little in volume, but are still murmurs. My mind wanders to family and friends, old friends from childhood. I smile at the memory of my teachers and my first car. A sense of completeness comes over me. I am no longer curious or confused. I am only content. It is all I need to be. A voice, my mother's.

"How are you?"

"I'm content."

"Good. Listen more."

I focus on the murmurs. The more I listen, the more distinct the voices become, but no individual words. I can hear men, women, children. I can discern faces and places. The sound of children laughing. Someone is playing a piano. Cars are honking. There is the roar of a jet plane taking off. I can see my mother walking on the sidewalk holding my hand on my first day of school. A building on fire collapses. There is more beautiful music, maybe Mozart. I sense how much Beth loved me and I loved her. I see the gentle ripples on the pond.

"Son, why don't you open your eyes and be with us again?"

I open my eyes and am back on the park bench. Dazed. My mother asks if I am okay.

"Yes. What was happening?"

"You were tapping into the collective experiences, the sensations of everyone."

"I'm not sure how to ask this, but how deep into the collective consciousness did I get?"

My father practically snorts. "Hardly at all. You were probably picking up old memories, yours and others of the prior life. That's how everyone starts. After a while you learn to pay attention to what is important."

"Which is..."

"The spirit of God and the spirit of people."

"I got a little of that."

"No," my mom said. "If you did, you wouldn't have come back when we asked you to."

"Really?"

"Really."

"It was unbelievable."

My dad wants to explain more. "What you experienced is a bare beginning. Memories are comforting, having a physical presence seems normal. This is what you experienced. But you soon learn what is important. It is the essence of people, of God, that you will treasure. That is possible only in the collective consciousness. It is the oneness of God."

"And that's what you experience all the time."

"Yes. All the time, forever."

"No need to remember your prior life, people you loved."

"All that is like the wind. Here, and then gone."

My mother tried to wax poetic. But I understand what she meant. The prior life, the one I left only a few days ago, was insignificant. For my mom and dad, the only reason for awareness was to be connected to God. An individual self was not necessary to connect. In fact, it appeared the only way to connect was for everyone to be part of everyone. One being, including God. I get it.

"How long does it take?"

"Does it matter?"

"No, I suppose not. Can everybody manage it?"

"Everyone can manage it. You get help."

I had to smile. "Yeah. I understand, you get help. But Dad, I've got to ask you this. What's the point?"

"What's the point?"

"Yeah. What's the purpose of doing this; the same thing forever?"

"Ah, the purpose of Heaven."

That tone of voice. I recognize it. We're reverting to debate mode. This will be fun. My dad and I could grab any subject and shake it like a bulldog into its smallest parts to make a point. We didn't argue, we didn't ever fight, at least after my teenage years, but boy did we debate.

"Yes. What's the point of your Heavenly existence?" I threw down the gauntlet.

"You, of anyone, should understand. Let me ask you a question. When you were in college, and after, well into middle age, you were a staunch environmentalist. Right?"

"Yes, and proud to be one."

"And I recall you talking about and contributing time and money to help elephants survive. Is that right?"

"They were being poached into extinction."

"So what?"

"What do you mean, 'so what?'"

"Who cares if they become extinct?"

"What's that got to do with what we're talking about,

the purpose of Heaven?"

"A lot. Just answer the question."

My dad is crafty and setting up to pounce. My poor mother is sitting between us, normally a horrible spot to be. But I imagine she is also in the middle of the collective consciousness so it doesn't matter where she sits.

"Okay. 'Who cares if they become extinct?' The world. The balance of nature. It's doing the right thing. Elephants have every right to live."

"For what purpose?"

"What do you mean 'for what purpose?'"

"What's the point to their existence?"

What was the purpose of an elephant's life? Ask any elephant and they couldn't tell you. To create more elephants didn't seem to answer the question, only made it a larger question. Balance of nature? Nature was rebalancing itself all the time. Heck, ninety-nine percent of species that ever lived went extinct. What's one more extinction? Is simply being alive the point?

"The point is, Dad, that being alive allows an infinity of possibilities."

"To what end? What's the point of one possibility or an infinity of possibilities? What difference does it make?"

"You're saying life doesn't need to have a point?"

My Dad leans toward me and smiles. "What I'm leading to is that life should have a purpose, as should the afterlife, but they are not the same purpose."

"Oh."

"Shall I explain?"

"Please."

"Life has no guarantees. Take the average Joe. Works

hard and occasionally wins on poker night. But he also might suffer a flat tire on the drive home. Life isn't easy. Joe has to figure out ways forward and upward every day. He will connect with people and count on them. He won't connect with others and worry they will stab him in the back. For the average Joe, the point to life is to make today okay and tomorrow better in all the ways that can be done. Agree?"

"Sounds good."

"The afterlife is different. The struggle has ended. The purpose isn't to make today okay and tomorrow better. The purpose of the afterlife is to experience salvation. That's what we do, all the time."

"There's nothing more to accomplish?"

"Not a thing."

"Mom?"

"Dear, what your father said is right. There are no needs to meet. No chores or obligations. That was before. Life was a struggle, a good struggle, a rewarding struggle. We didn't make the right decisions all the time and had to make adjustments here and there. We were generally happy, but sometimes had to endure sad events. All that is gone now. And we're not in an eternal rest, vegging out as people might say. That would be ridiculous. We're experiencing rapture. That's the point."

"You're wondering if even this gets boring. Are you?" My dad asks.

"Well, I wonder about sameness, nothing changing. Seems too much like a constant drug high. You can get that from the right mushrooms; just eat them often enough."

"To understand the difference, change your reference

from having a physical body to not having one. With a body you live in a world of experiences, any of which would become boring after a while, drug induced or scoring a winning touchdown induced. Too much of anything is too much. Agreed?"

"Yes, agreed."

"Without a body, everything changes. There is no too much, no habituation to anything. There is no grabbing an experience and holding on to it until another comes along. Awareness is a flow. It doesn't matter if the experience, if the sensation, is changing or constant. Now I don't know if this is true, but it makes sense. It may be that we each keep a part of ourselves within the collective consciousness. We each may experience what others are experiencing, that might keep it fresh too."

I admit all he said rang true. The old man still has it.

"Well Dad and Mom, it seems like you are where you want to be."

"That's right," they say together as they fade into the ether. With their exit, I make mine.

Pete points to the coffee table. Waiting for me are a Jumbo Jack with cheese, a large chocolate shake and a lemon pie, my favorite meal when I was in graduate school. He has the same.

"Well?" he asks as we sit and plow into the finest fast food ever created.

"More questions, Pete, than I have answers. I met God; that was nice. Took part, a little, in the collective consciousness, saw my folks, experienced weightlessness, sat under a tree by a pond."

"You make it sound almost ordinary."

"If you're into eternal salvation it has to be the most profound experience and it isn't even experience, it is everything. Heaven was totality. Everything is one with God. There is nothing else but unity and total love. Yet, I like being me, just me and what I do and experience."

"You're still measuring Heaven by your earthly life and how you created meaning there."

"I know."

"Still want to die?"

"I think so."

"How sure are you?"

"Truthfully, not sure."

"Big decision."

"Yeah."

We focus on our dinner. I can remember when this meal was hardly enough to last me until dinnertime. Now I am slowing half way through the burger and the milkshake and I won't make it to the lemon pie. Pete isn't having that problem and I don't doubt he'll ask if he can have my pie.

I have a choice now. After I make it, I will have no more choices. Sure would be easier to leave the choice up to the almighty. It's either God, dimensions or me to make the decision. Which is best equipped? I have only the experience of one life. I don't have omniscience, infinite wisdom or the computing power of thousands of dimensions. But the one life I had was mine. The one death was mine. The hereafter should be mine too. That must mean something; but what? I don't want to give up me, but if I die, I give up me. Reminds me of the Vietnam War saying, "We had to destroy the village in order to save it from the communists." I could talk with a thousand wise people in Heaven and learn from them. And, God or the dimensions would comprehend more than a hundred thousand wise people. But they're not me.

Dread should be overtaking me now. It's not.

My life had meaning because I could contribute. It also gave me meaning because I loved and was loved. I don't think I contribute anything in Heaven; there is no need to contribute except my own. But Heaven, on the other hand, is total love forever. But, isn't love more precious when it is fragile and can be lost? In Heaven I can't have both contributing and love as I did in my earthly life. What do I value more, to contribute or to have everlasting love? What is it to be human? Do I give that up to be in Heaven?

Pete looks at me with the expression every parent has seen. I slide my pie over to his side.

As he unwraps the pie he says, "Enough thinking and pondering and wondering." He nods to the nearby wall. "Let's take in a movie."

I look toward the wall where a large screen television now hangs. We watch Billy Wilder's "Some Like It Hot" with Tony Curtis, Marilyn Monroe and Jack Lemon, and then call it a night.

Day
10

Final Exit

My eyes are closed. I don't want to fully wake up. The bed is too soft, too comfortable, too welcoming to vacate just yet. Yesterday had been more than I expected, and I had expected a lot. To experience God's Heaven, my version anyway, to be with my parents, to talk with God, to be part of the collective consciousness, was a revelation. I truly expected something akin to sitting on a cloud listening to harp music. And I don't accept all of it was of my making. Little of that could have been in my head. Maybe some, but this had authenticity beyond my imagination and was compelling. It was real. That was God's Heaven, not my conception.

Heaven doesn't have the same purpose as the prior life. That is true. The only purpose is to fulfill God's desire to express love, and to receive it, and to share it. This morning the question remains: Do I want that?

Pete is coming over for brunch, bringing juice, coffee and Danish. I don't know how I know, but I do and it's no longer surprising I do. Contentment is still solid throughout my being. Curiosity waning. Confusion about gone. Heaven's three Cs are morphing into one C, contentment. My parents said they were experiencing the big S, salvation. Upon death, I had been expecting the big N, nothingness. And I no longer feel dread. I'm comfortable with my decision since it no longer matters if God made Heaven or the multiple dimensions did.

I shave as I always do and take a long shower, longer than usual. The water temperature is perfect and the flow strong enough to beat a pleasant massage on my head. I pull on khakis, a polo shirt and loafers without socks and walk out on the pool deck to greet the day. I have a little preparing to do.

Pete arrives about ten minutes after I finish, bringing brunch as I anticipated. After handing me a cup of coffee, he spreads the Danish on a plate and places two glasses of cranberry juice on the table.

The sun has been up for a few hours warming the air, which is clear enough to suggest the mountains had moved thirty miles closer during the night. Birds are chirping nearby. Perfect brunch weather and brunch setting.

"What's up?" Pete asks, munching on a raspberry Danish.

I explain the day and my conclusion that if God exists, he created a great Heaven. Pete responds saying that fact wasn't in question. I had been experiencing Heaven for the past nine days. God or no God, this is Heaven and it is perfect. But Pete looks different.

"Have you changed?"

"What do you mean?"

"You look different. Darker skin, sharper features."

"I've been changing my genetic makeup ten percent a day after the first day."

"Why would you do that?"

"Just for fun and to see if anyone noticed. I started out a California boy, like you. Second day I added from the gene pool of the Sudan. I was ninety percent California and ten percent Sudanese. After that, one day and ten percent at a time I added Norway, Japan, Saudi Arabia, Australia, Argentina, Ukraine, China, and last, Native American. Now I'm ten percent California and ninety percent other stuff."

"Aren't I the only one who sees you? I had no idea."

"Yes, you're the only one. I think Native American added just the right touch to my features for you to see a difference. And earlier you were busy with personal matters. Just experimenting and having fun, man."

"Son of a gun. I didn't notice. You've become a one person melting pot. And I know that voice was Maynard G. Krebs."

As we finish brunch, except for a few last sips of coffee, I bring up the project I want to do.

"Pete, ever create a mandala?"

"I'm not sure what you're asking."

I point out containers of colored sand I had conjured. "We draw images and patterns on the deck with chalk and fill them in with colored sand. We put the sand in a funnel to sprinkle on the designs. Buddhist monks create intricate designs and maybe two, three, four or more of them take a week or two making it, then take it apart and pour the sand into a stream or let the wind and rain do the job to symbolize the circle of life. I figure we can do a simple one together that won't take too long."

"Is it religion or art?"

"For them religious. For us, a joint project to symbolize what we're doing."

"What's the design?"

"Only outlined. Come take a look."

We get up and walk twenty-feet to where I had stored the plastic containers of sand. Off to the side on the pool deck I had drawn a chalk circle about five-feet in diameter. With two vertical lines I had divided the circle into three sections of about equal size.

"Pete, this symbolizes what you and I are doing. The left section is my prior life. The middle section is the present and the right-hand section is what comes next. We design each section and fill in with sand. Should take three or four hours and when the time comes we can dump the sand in the grass. You game?"

"Sounds great. How do we proceed?"

"I can define the prior life part and we can mutually decide how to represent it. You define the middle part and we'll mutually figure out the design. For the last part, we wing it."

"And you want work in that sequence, life, now, later. Okay, start us off."

For my prior life, I tell Pete, the design should include, at the least, falling in love, raising a family, trying and failing, trying and succeeding, nature, playing, sharing, helping others, cats and dogs, and education. We have a great time discussing what symbolizes what and what color would best represent what we're depicting. There are plenty of colors, nine different ones and if we're careful, we can combine two colors into a third. Plastic squeeze bottles prove easier to use than funnels. We start after agreeing on one symbol, a red heart imbedded with five small circles, symbolizing my childhood family. After outlining and filling it in, examining our work, redoing what had to be improved, looking again and deciding what would fit in next, we add two lines upwards and two lines downwards to represent the family members that came before and those that would come after. It looks good.

The second design we put in is about the earth, nature, water, trees, animals. We start with a sphere, coloring it with green, blue and brown sand in wavy lines. To represent life we add an abstract tree on the left. We don't want real images of things, but we decide we'll put that in and see if we still like it later. Quite a few times we try something we don't like and encounter the problem of cleaning up the sand without disturbing what we had already done. An electric hand vacuum is handy, but that doesn't seem to be in the spirit of our task and decide not to use it. Creating a vacuum with a rubber bulb to suck up the sand doesn't work well. We end up blotting the sand with a wet paper towel and drying the spot before trying another design.

The first section takes about three hours. As we finish, Pete says he has an idea and asks me to put a tiny smiley face in the lowest portion of the section. I must squeeze it next to an upside down triangle representing growing old, but it fits pretty well. Pete is deft keeping the sand within the designs where I am clumsy so he adds two tiny eyes and the mouth. The image is small; the eyes take only three or four grains of sand. It's a beautiful smiley face. As he finishes, Pete looks up and asks, "Was it worth it?"

"Was what worth it?"

"Life. Was it worth living?"

"As opposed to not living at all?"

"Yes."

How would I judge that? A life with more good than bad? Highs so wonderful no bad could diminish them? How can I compare life to nonlife? What was life *supposed* to be, if it was supposed to be anything in the first place? If I somehow had a choice, would I choose to experience life? I chose not to die while I lived, does that mean anything?

"Pete, I thought you were supposed to help me."

"I am helping you."

"Some people say life is a not-very-funny cosmic joke."

"What do you say?"

Pete watches silently as I think about his question. Then it becomes clear. Perhaps all my searching about the meaning of life clouded the simplicity of the matter. Yeah, my life was worth living I half say to myself.

Pete rises from his kneeling position.

"Yes," I tell him. "My life was worth living."

"Do you want to thank anyone for it?"

"...Actually...no, I don't. It wasn't my choice one way or another. And I ended up responsible whether or not I wanted to be. But I liked it."

"Glad to hear it. By the way," he says. "You're ready."

"Ready for what?"

"To spread your wings. Gorge on the enchilada grando. Punch the big ticket. You're ready for the whole of Heaven. Today is your last day here."

"I like it here."

"Of course you like it here, it's Heaven."

"How do you know I'm ready?"

"I will tell you. You spent the first couple of days getting used to being dead and in Heaven. Then you explored some of the highs and lows of earthly life, from slam dunks to racial tensions and atomic bombs. People often do that at first, return to earthly things; like a child watching the same movie ten times. After that, you enjoyed a perfect day, something that could be repeated for infinity and make a decent Heaven. You experienced a version of God's Heaven. Now I find you symbolically capturing your life and afterlife journey, closing the book in a way to your worth-living prior existence. You're ready to join your ancestors, and everybody else."

"You have enough data?"

"Elegant in its symmetry; you're ready for Heaven, Heaven is ready for you."

"Do I have to go right now?"

"Not at all."

"I can go when I want?"

"Sure. We can finish the mandala. We can enjoy a tasty supper and catch the sunset. Whatever suits your fancy."

"How is it done? How do I go on from here?"

"If you agree, we can do the door thing again. Open the door, take one step, time stops and you enter paradise."

"One step, time stops, paradise. Hmm."

"You recall my telling you about time around here. It's different. Time stopping is a big deal."

"All right. Thanks for telling me I'm ready. I'd like to do what you mentioned. Finish the mandala, enjoy dinner and the sunset, preferably with a Scotch."

"Done. Let's get back to work."

Pete decides the middle section should include a bed, a clock, two human figures or representations, the ocean, the Heavenly ether, the big bang, a coffee cup, sunset and whatever else comes to mind. This one also takes three hours but for good reason; we're faster because we're better at spreading the sand, but slower because we now can produce better looking symbols and we take our time to do so.

The third section we will design as we go. We stop for iced tea and discuss our ideas while we relax in the pool chairs. Pete waits for me to start.

"I want to represent a finale, the end point of the journey; something definite, something good, not uncertain or magical. I don't want any religious items that would define a specific religion. It has to be inclusive, somehow representing forever. And it has to be different from the prior life one.

"Oh. Why don't you give us something hard?"

"Sorry. What do you think should be in it?" I figure Pete might drop a few hints about what the next step will be like.

"Emotions. Sense of joy, completeness, contentment, salvation, calm, optimism, or nothingness, meaning the absence of good and bad, and the absence of time and space."

"Pete, can you describe what I'll experience when I get the full deal?"

"It is beyond your wildest imagination. No way for me to describe it."

"I wondered. I'm also wondering if we should leave the last section of the mandala blank. Why put something in that has no relevance to what it really is?"

"Good point. Are the other two sections what you want?"

"Almost. I liked the smiley face in the first section representing death. A smiley face epitomizing death; who would have thought of that? What I want to do in the second section is add another smiley face. That will represent you, not death, but life in the afterlife."

"I would be honored to be a smiley face in your mandala of the afterlife."

We team up again, me doing the round yellow face and Pete doing the eyes and mouth.

As we consider our work, Pete has another idea.

"Do you want to represent your hopes about Heaven in the third section? You don't have to represent Heaven; you could put in what you expect."

"Actually, I want to erase the outline of that section and have only the two, prior life and the initial Heaven. Both those sections are real to me."

"If you don't mind my saying so, the whole of Heaven deserves to be part of the picture even if that picture isn't yet complete."

"I'd rather leave it as it is, as nothing. I like that. I don't have to be aware of everything now. Will I know everything later?"

"You bet."

"That's sounds real good. My contentment meter just pegged at maximum. I like the mandala, thanks for helping."

"You're welcome."

"I can put together supper. My plan is fish and chips again, and peas. A nice cod and a nice dry Chardonnay. What do you say?"

"I say count me in."

Over dinner, we discuss free will and collective consciousness. In my parent's Heaven, they had little or no free will. They were part of everyone. They were as happy and fulfilled as anyone could be. The sense of contentment was total. What could be wrong with that? What could be wrong is the loss of self, of individuality and the ability to make independent decisions. After a fifteen-minute discourse, I end with as concise a summary of me as I can manage.

"I'm a simple guy, Pete, not important in the grand scheme of things. Do I throw my fate into the collective consciousness to be lost in the cacophony of everyone's thoughts and feelings or be true to my individuality and face my end with dignity?"

"Sounds like you're still in a hurry."

"I don't get what you mean."

"That cacophony you described, all those thoughts and voices at once. God's included. Sure, it's a big mess. You'd be lost. You may as well be a cork in the ocean. What if it took ten-thousand years to make your voice heard to billions of others? But you eventually connect with all of them and all of them connect with you. Would that be worth the wait? Knowing you could do that from then on?"

"I suppose it's okay that the collective consciousness would take getting used to. I wouldn't be a cork in the ocean forever."

"Mike, one last time. It wouldn't take getting used to. There is no time passing."

"Got it, got it, got it. There's more though. Life, the concept of life. To me, life is growing, changing, striving for something. There is nothing like that in Heaven. I'm back to what's the purpose?"

"Okay, growing, striving, all part of life. Life is survival. Life is making it one more day. Heaven means not having to strive anymore. You have everything. Heaven is the time to rejoice."

"Yeah, I heard that before; eternal rejoicing. At least I'm getting the same message. But there's more.

"Of course there's more. Let's scrutinize everything. Speaking of scrutinizing everything, I suggest we adjourn to the pool deck with your favorite Scotch to enjoy the sunset."

We rise from the table, leaving the dishes for later.

"Gosh, this is my last meal. Is that right?"

"Probably, but not necessarily."

"My last meal. That's weird. I don't feel like a condemned man, but that's what it's like. How many people know they're eating their last meal? Let's grab that drink and sit outside to enjoy my last sunset."

I get the Scotch bottle while Pete fills two glasses with ice and we head outside.

"Had you realized that was your last meal earlier,

would you have had something different?"

"No. The last of anything from my prior life isn't all that important."

By the time we sit, the sun is reaching the top of the mountains. We haven't missed a thing. I continue my last minute sorting of issues.

"I want to raise the concept of contributing. I realize in Heaven we don't need to contribute, but I like doing that. I'd go as far as saying I need to do that. Isn't Heaven supposed to meet my needs?"

"You're assuming you have the same need to contribute in Heaven as you did before?"

"Doing it again, huh?"

"Not exactly. Heaven will meet all your needs. There is life and there is afterlife. Two different things. Apples and oranges."

We're silent as the sun drops to touch the mountains and begins the silent explosion of pink and red behind them. Here I am, sipping my favorite Scotch, conversing with a learned friend of ten days, discussing the joys of life and the potential of Heaven, after a satisfying meal, relaxed, part of a glorious sunset. I love sunsets.

"Doesn't get any better than this," I say.

Pete turns to me and smiles, that happy, engaging smile of his. "Don't be so sure."

"Okay, returning to what we were talking about, contributing. I have a lot to contribute. I'm not done yet. I died, I accept that. But like most people, I died too early; I still had the ability to improve things. Why waste all the benefit of my experience and willingness?"

"Why me, God?"

"No, not why me. In a way, I'm asking why anybody. Every minute earth loses good people."

"Got it. You're thinking people should die the moment they run out of gas and can't contribute anymore. Right?"

"When you put it that way, and you're right, sounds ridiculous."

"But there is a better way to understand what happens. Earth is a process, getting better all the time. You did your part, allow others to do theirs."

Now a tenth of the sky is a brilliant red. Near where the sun is disappearing behind the mountains is a bright yellow, turning gold and then pink. I continue.

"Pete, so far so good. You are being helpful."

"Thank you. All part of the job."

"You've mentioned time a lot; making sure I understand that time is different here. Has time stopped already? Doesn't seem like it."

"You've experienced days because that helps you adjust. Time has passed for you in this room and elsewhere. Time will not exist for you later. It isn't necessary. Time is useful only if you are doing something or going somewhere. In Heaven you're not doing anything in the normal sense of the word and you're not going anywhere either. There is no space and time ceases to exist. It's a hard concept to get your mind around. Think about you and Professor Einstein observing the big bang. That began without time or space. Why not Heaven? It might be understandable if we both were math geniuses, but I'm sure not."

"Me either, but I trust what you're saying."

The sky is welcoming night.

"Other issues?" Pete asks.

"Only a few. But, I want to understand everything. Back to free will for a moment. In the expanded Heaven I will enter, I will be aware that I am in Heaven?"

"Yes."

"I will know I have choices?"

"Yes. You can go any place you like. You might return here and make me another dinner or return to earth in some form. You could create your own version of Heaven. Anything you like."

"To be clear, I can end my existence if I want to, whenever I want to."

"Yes."

"And I will know how to do that?

"Yes."

I search for any anxiety, or dread. I find only a deep contentment.

"And the real version of Heaven, the whole enchilada, awaits me through the door?"

"As I said, my friend, it will be perfect for you. You will get all you want, and much more. Let me put it this way. In the past ten days, we've discussed many topics and you've had your questions answered. You've experienced a Heaven as an ideal life and enjoyed that. You went to a Heaven you envisioned God would create and learned from your parents that such a place was beyond belief. Now you have a chance to discover what true Heaven is like, a perfect Heaven for you. Are you ready?"

Stars are dotting the night sky. They're beautiful. Time to go.

"Yes I am."

I down my drink and take the glass into the kitchen.

Pete and I walk to the door. I open it, turn, and shake Pete's hand. It was a strong handshake, more intimate than a hug. We didn't move our hands up and down, but shook in the modern way, clasping the other, neither moving, neither trying to squeeze harder, but to hold onto the others hand in a manly embrace. We touch one another not unlike Michelangelo's Sistine Chapel portrayal of God's finger touching Adam. It was a stark reminder of being alive, one person touching and being touched by another, a feeling I hadn't had in a while. It was a whisper from the past. I smile as I think of the unfinished mandala and let go of his hand.

"Thank you, Pete."

"My pleasure, Mike."

"Take one step forward," he says. "Time will stop and you will enter paradise."

Dread is gone. After all that pondering, I finally got it into my concrete head that the meaning of my earthly life, my purpose of contributing did not have to be my purpose in heaven. Heaven could have a new purpose. And my earthly goal of touching and being touched could be substituted for love in all its glory. Having a choice made the difference. I am no longer curious; no longer confused. I am content. I move to the door and open it, and take the step without looking back.

"Whoa."

Book Club Discussion Questions

We all must comprehend what our personal mortality means. For some death is the end, for others it is the beginning of an eternal afterlife. No one knows. The scientifically minded point to no evidence of God and growing evidence that many religious stories cannot be true. The faithful rely on unshakable faith. The following questions may open a discussion, one that is not designed to convert anyone one way or the other, but to explore how religion and secularism can coexist without harming anyone.

Book clubs might find value choosing two or three questions to discuss while individual readers might benefit from pondering a question while sitting next to a fire sipping a favorite beverage.

1. Much to his surprise, Mike arrived in Heaven. He eventually liked the idea that Heaven was for everyone. Whom do you think should be allowed in?

2. Heaven is only for the self-aware, leaving out young infants and the unborn. People could allow these young ones into their version of Heaven. How early in biological development should they accept, all the way back to a fertilized egg?

3. What do you think happens to those who arrive in Heaven with special circumstances such as someone with Down syndrome, schizophrenia, sociopathy or blindness?

4. Why did the author declare that both a Pope and

Hitler would take the same time (six hours) to enter Heaven? Do they represent similar type groups somehow?

5. Why might it be good or bad to give up individuality to join the collective consciousness?

6. Should you be aware you're in Heaven?

7. If you had the opportunity in Heaven, what people would you visit?

8. Whose minds would you like to share?

9. Should there be both Heaven and Hell?

10. There are many religions that foster the idea that those in Heaven can help those on earth. Why should that be the case; or should it?

11. What effect would there be on earthly religions if intelligent, self-aware alien life forms can enter Heaven, or if they even exist?

12. Mike spent part of his time in Heaven experiencing or observing various earthly people activity such as playing professional basketball, driving while black and listening to President Lincoln deliver the Gettysburg Address. What would you have done?

13. What went wrong in the driving while black situation? How could this have been prevented?

14. How can Mike deny the existence of God yet accept the existence of over 11,000 dimensions? And why so many dimensions; a hundred would

have been enough.

15. Mike seemed to change during his first ten days. Did he become a believer before entering the final Heaven?

16. Should earthy life and Heavenly life have a purpose? If so, what should it be?

17. What did Mike want in Heaven? Did he get it?

18. Will Mike be able to end his existence if he wishes?

19. Why wouldn't God simply reveal Himself or Herself or Itself?

20. If an afterlife exists, why should death occur? Why not everlasting life from the start?

Acknowledgements

First to thank is my wife Deena who rises after the alarm goes off at five most days. She brings home the bacon while I spend the day enjoying the agony of writing.

I normally thank my editor(s) at this point but must acknowledge that for the first time editing was done through a collection of editing software. I thought this would add a new dimension to the work. Later I realized this would be a mistake and asked Jill Corley to be my editor. Her touch was magic.

A few beta readers had a hand in improving the quality of the story and the writing. From jolly England Emma made her contribution and from sunny Jamaica Nat added her ideas. My brother-in-law Danny, who reads most of my books, added his wisdom for the small cost of being served drinks on the back deck. My friend and go to reader Brian Weisel read a later version, found some errors and weak spots as he always seems to do and helped me improve the effort.

About the Author

Bob Brown is the president of Collective Wisdom, Inc. a consulting company that helps improve people interactions. He is the author of nineteen books and numerous articles. He and his wife live north of Seattle, Washington with a few animals, wild and domestic, which currently includes moles in the back yard.

Like Mike, the meaning of my life comes from the effort to contribute. Some of the material in *My First Ten Days of Heaven* is from *Personal Wisdom: Making Sense of You, Others and the Meaning of Life* and the memoir *Simply Bob*. The challenge was to present important tools and concepts of life in an easily digestible story. I hope I at least partially succeeded.

You might also enjoy:

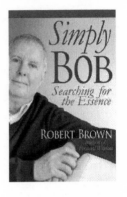

The story of Bob's search for the meaning of life. Bob's life was shattered in under seven seconds. It wasn't illness or accident. It was a documentary movie in high school and it took him forty years to recover.

(from chapter one)

On May twenty-first, 1946, at Mercy Hospital in Ann Arbor, Michigan, at a decent hour and with dispatch, I entered the scene. I knew right from the start that I was okay; it was the rest of the world that worried me.

World War II had just ended. In fact, President Harry Truman didn't officially declare the end of the war until I was seven months old. Other events of this auspicious time included: Emperor Hirohito of Japan declared that he wasn't a god; people paid ten cents for a loaf of bread while the minimum wage was forty cents an hour; the US military was racially segregated; and one of the best songs on the Hit Parade was "The Gypsy" by the Ink Spots.

Growing up in the middle of it all was me, asking questions and looking for answers. I wanted to use my turn wisely yet in the background my personal clock was already ticking. How best to live my allotted days? Does life, especially human life, have an essence, some quality that makes it special? Is the meaning of life personal or is it the same for everyone? This is my account of what I eventually figured out.

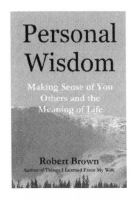

Personal Wisdom

Making Sense of You Others and the Meaning of Life

Robert Brown
Author of Things I Learned From My Wife

Bob's ideas, tips and tools to live an absolutely wonderful life.

(from chapter one)

Life is a mystery. None of us did anything to make it happen. Without warning, we slip into life one day, struggle to make our way through it, and eventually stop living, sometimes while we're still alive.

We are made of cosmic dust from a biochemical recipe handed down from a million years ago. And although the ingredients are the same, the recipe has infinite variations.

Each of us is unique, yet similar to all. We see the same night sky as our grandparents and dream the same dreams as the pharaohs. Parts of me are identical to parts of you. We feel the same pain, the same joys, and ask the same questions.

But we don't follow the same paths. You know things I don't. You grasp ideas I wouldn't understand. I have struggled where you succeed in an instant, and you have created a list of accomplishments that would amaze me.

We come in all sizes, shapes, IQs, races, nationalities, attitudes, temperaments, and just about everything else. What we all have in common is this experience we call life. Some see it as a burden, others a gift. What your life ultimately is depends on you.

If for no other reason, your life is precious because it will end. Before it ends, whether this is a long time or all too brief, you have the opportunity to decide how to define your life and what should be done with it. Life isn't so much what you experience as what you decide.

Bob learned early and often that a wife has wisdom beyond a man's under-standing.

(from chapter one)

It's a fact that men don't under-stand women. We do everything else that can be imagined with them, worship, torment, ignore, embarrass, hurt, love, hate, adore; you name it, we do it. Usually we don't know why. Most relationships men have with women are shoot-from-the-hip affairs. Whatever we do makes sense at the time, if not the next morning.

Men are biologically driven to want only one thing. Once we get that thing, we're satisfied for a time until we have the urge to get that one thing again. The thing we want doesn't require much skill, or intelligence, grace, dignity, or much of anything except a willing partner, preferably a smooth skinned, curvaceous, red-lipped nymphomaniac, at least some of the time anyway.

Women fit into a man's understanding of the world as a convenience. A woman in the same room when he wants the one thing is better than a woman down the hall or across town. All the better if that woman also brings a tray full of snacks and a can of beer during the football game.

A dark story of evil, revenge, and remorse where only the ultimate sacrifice can keep a promise.

(from chapter one)

"Do you want to start a fight?" Harold finally asked, his face tight.

"No," Shelly answered. "I don't want to start a fight. I want to start a family."

He sighed. "We've been over this a thousand times. The risk is too great now. It's unfair to bring someone into the world with no opportunity for a real life."

"What about being unfair to me and to us?" Shelly stood up from the table and blew out the candles. She silently began to collect the dishes, scraping leftover scampi into a bowl.

"Shelly, I am being fair to you, and to us. We'll have a child when the chances are in our favor, not the opposite. I'm not against having children. You know that. I know you want children. So do I."

She stopped to look at him. "I don't know that," she insisted. "I don't know that you want children. I don't know that you would accept whatever we would get. And even if our child didn't have a genetic defect, it might have something else wrong."

Harold was quiet. She was well aware of the probabilities. Why would she bring this up now?

As she stacked the dirty dishes, Shelly continued. "Even a short life is better than none. Life has no guarantees. Not ever. Honey, to see one sunrise, to hear one nightingale, to smell one rose, to fall in love one time. If that's all you can have, that's enough. It isn't the length. It's what is experienced and what can be shared..."

Golf before the turn of the last century: Couples, Norman and Faldo in their prime, Kevin Turner playing his heart out on and off the course, Foot buying distilleries and Oscar Brown listening to the voices.

(from the preface)

The northeast corner of Fife is not like the rugged high cliffs of the Scottish west coast, but is mostly gently rolling farmland wandering haphazardly into the sea. Layered rocks exposed by centuries of storms rise to greet gray waves that surge in endless rows toward shore.

A blanket of clouds hung in tatters as young Oscar Brown walked along the shoreline footpath, a narrow strip of packed dirt hugging the slope between shore rocks and farm fields. He was distracted by two gulls squawking over a dead herring that bobbed in the gentle swell. Their shrill cries invited a dozen more gulls. The largest one, unblemished white with a patch of red on his yellow beak, swooped down, snatched the herring and flew toward the open sea, chased by a shrieking string of also-rans.

Oscar's wind-chapped cheeks were used to the spring chill, so too his small and calloused hands. A sweater was all he needed, but he wore a coat to conceal the revolver he had taken from his father's cabinet that morning. The thick wool absorbed the sea breeze as he abandoned the path to scramble among the rocks.

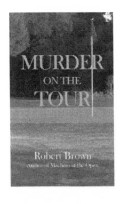

Tour golf with a few murders, a beautiful woman, a rich caddie and a desperate rookie.

(from the preface)

The Parkland was a cheap motel, the type commonly found just off secondary roads on the outskirts of almost any town. Named in honor of the rundown children's playground across the street it boasted two spindly Douglas Firs straddling the small cement porch of the check-in office. The chipped tile and the faded curtains told the story of an older couple's dream turning to dust. Eight bare rooms, an unrepaired icemaker, and a dirt parking lot made for low overhead for the smart new owner who knew how to squeeze out a hard buck. It was a haven for tired young families on a budget who happened on it late at night, independent salesmen who wanted privacy, and locals who sought an illicit pairing away from the eyes of town.

It proved perfect for the wallet of Tour caddies. The price was right with no charge for extra roommates. Bag carriers of famous golf professionals earn as much as a family doctor and stay in hotels with room service and dance floors, but the majority of caddies squeeze four or five together at a place like the Parkland and eat in the room or splurge at Benny's Bar-B-Q Burgers. Four rooms made a temporary home for at least a dozen caddies during tournament week.

Proof

Made in the USA
Columbia, SC
02 January 2018